MOCK'S BAD STOMP

MICKEY J. "MIKE" MARTIN

THE FOWBLE PRESS

MOCK'S BAD STOMP. Copyright© 2021 by Mickey J. "Mike" Martin. All rights reserved. Printed in the United States of America. No part of this book may be reproduced or utilized in any form or by any means, electronic or mechanical, including photocopying and recording, by any information storage and retrieval system, without permission of the author-publisher.

FIRST EDITION:
HARDBACK -- LARGE PRINT
ISBN 978-0-9638279-7-5
PAPERBACK - ISBN 978-0-9638279-8-2
(EPUB) -- 978-0-9638279-9-9
LCCN: 2021909316

MOCK'S BAD STOMP

CONTENTS

*****

FOREWORD

MOCK'S STORY BEGINS in the Oklahoma Indian Territory of the early 1800s and ends in the same area during the mid-1980s.

Any of a series of Burnham family life experiences as residents of their Creek Nation townsite out in the Territory could have been written about to draw attention to various historical injustices Native American people have had to endure in past years. An account of any one of those injustices would have made captivating and worthwhile reading, but a project of that kind is not the purpose of this effort. This narrative is meant to be much more specific and personal than an exposé of any one or the other category of problems among Indian people in general.

Instead, it is about the repercussions of a single tragic incident that took place during this period in our national history. Because only a limited amount of information was available about each of the key characters, this story of what happened to them is as lean and spare as an outline. Only enough information was recovered to recount the basic facts and illustrate how painfully true it is that people are seldom able to anticipate the consequences of major life events as they are happening. Etta Jane "Mock" Burnham certainly was not one of them; for her, getting by in life turned out to be a lot more than she knew how handle.

A FAMILY AT WAR

BOILING WITH ANGER, Andy Burnham boomed at his unruly daughter Etta: "You ain't ridin' in no damned wagon load of drunks over to them drunken stomps!" Although he was a full-blooded Creek Indian himself, his voice and argument and verbiage paralleled that of many if not most of the local whites of his time and place. A good number of whites were well known for spitting out these and other similarly derisive comments to express their unequivocal contempt for the Indian dances that were common in the area. Most of these events, as far as they were concerned, were a real problem in their part of the Territory. Andy could not have agreed more, not about stomps per se but for sure about many of those that had been going on in their vicinity. At some of them, things had gotten so far out of hand that he, along with a good number of his like-minded neighbors, white and Indian alike, were deeply upset about it.

For Andy Burnham or any other Indian father to object to a daughter going alone to one of these local events was not unusual. Public drunkenness at the dances had become so commonplace that the likelihood of a fistfight, stabbing, or shooting taking place wherever one was held was pretty much taken for granted. To sober-minded Andy, steering a kid — especially a daughter — away from any situation where problems of this kind might occur was a matter of ordinary common sense, which was precisely why he had forbidden Etta from going. His edict had gone over no better than any of his other dictates in recent years, and yet another full-blown argument had broken out between this weary father and his equally weary daughter. To him, it was a matter of principle; as a father, he had to do what ought to be done, which was to set his daughter straight.

Dismissing a communal get-together like the dance she wanted to attend as an unruly stomp was offensive to Etta, who thought it would be good fun and a great break from her humdrum existence. She did not think of it as a meaningless stomp, nor was she excessively concerned about the potential for problems breaking out while she was there. Ceremonial dances of its kind were traditional among the tribes of the Indian Territory, including Andy's own tribe, the Creeks. Violence at them was nothing more than another excuse for white disparagement of Indian activities. Railing over something that might never happen was, to her way of thinking, too pointless to take seriously.

Held at tribally sanctioned locations, tribal dances typically began at sunset and continued until sunrise, some of them lasting multiple days. They were of religious and ceremonial significance and socially important to tribes that put them on and, to be fair, most of them were orderly and well managed. The Green Corn Festival, for example, was so popular that people from all around turned out to take it in.

Unfortunately, too many local dances had disintegrated to such a low point that there was no way that they could be referred to as being well managed. Ceremonial significance had proven not to be enough to prevent behavior from getting out of hand at them, sometimes on a regular basis. Most dances went off without incident, while others, regrettably, did not.

Andy had reached his wit's end during this latest conflagration with what he considered his shamelessly quarrelsome daughter. It was only the most recent in what had become a seemingly never-ending series of increasingly bitter arguments between them. Truth be known, their immediate argument was nothing new; battles between them had been going on for years. Once again, he had ended up utterly bewildered by the reality of his relationship with Etta. It had clearly disintegrated to the point of her not showing an iota of respect for his authority as a father.

There just ain't no talkin' to that girl! was the refrain that never stopped coursing through his mind. Andy knew that his own ass would have been beaten raw had he ever railed against his father the way his daughter routinely did with him. His dad had been about as old school as they come. He had learned the hard way that it was impossible to reason with the man. If he had ever bucked against his father, he knew there would have been hell to pay.

He bestowed Mock as a nickname upon Etta,

thinking that it was an excellent fit her aggravating tendency to ridicule or mock the directions any authority figure gave her. That included mocking the legitimate commands of her own father — in reality, especially the commands of her father.

"You know," he had exclaimed to her in the heat of a past moment, "you can't hardly talk if you ain't mockin' somebody. You do it so damned much that your name ought to be Mock instead of Etta." After giving the matter a little more thought, he latched onto the idea. "That's what I'm gonna do," he said; "I'm gonna start callin' you Mock." And from that point forward, that's exactly what Andy did. For him, it was more a means of driving home a point than anything else. Regardless of the reasoning behind it, the nickname quickly caught on. Within a few years, nearly every person in the community had begun calling her Mock as well. They, too, thought the appellation was an excellent fit.

"You know as well as I do," he bellowed at his belligerent daughter, "there ain't been nothin' but trouble at them stomps. Puttin' your butt out there right in the damned big middle of a drunken mess like one of them sure as hell ain't nothin' but askin' for trouble. You been doin' a whole hell of a lot of that lately, damned if you haven't!"

"Keep it up, gal," he raged, "and you're gonna wind up in more trouble than you know what to do with. You ain't nearly as smart as you think you are, by God! You got an attitude on you that won't don't. If you run your mouth off over there like you do at home with me and your momma, one of them bucks out there is liable to bust it wide open!"

"Oh, yes, I am goin' to 'them damned stomps,' as you call them," Mock screamed back at him. She was a young woman who had a long history for no discernible rhyme or reason on all sorts of occasions for resisting all legitimate authority — parental, communal, or otherwise. It had been her way for as long as anyone could remember, starting during her early childhood years and continuing all the way up to the present.

It was well established that at every opportunity, Mock would end up becoming a behavioral problem. Not a soul in her immediate family or, for that matter, in the community at large, including Mock herself, could explain why. For better or worse, that was the way she always was. She had been that way since her earliest years, and lately her negative behavior had grown even more pronounced. No one knew what to with her.

Now that she was a few years past the age at which most girls in her extended family or, for that matter, in the general area, left home to launch households of their own, Mock's belligerent disrespectfulness had increased to the point of turning it into a veritable suit of armor. Extremely impertinent behavior had become something of a hammer for her — a tool for fighting back against an environment she hated and an atmosphere she desperately wanted to, in her own words, get the hell out of for good. If she could only find her own job or someone to stay with, she swore to herself on a regular basis, I'd get out of my parents' place so damned fast that their thick, stupid heads would spin right off their shoulders!

"You sure are gettin' a big mouth on you, girl, talkin' back to your daddy like you do!" her mother Ruby, whose anger with her obstinate daughter was nearly — but not quite — the equal of her husband's, had chimed in. "Carryin' on the way you do is why you're goin' on 20 years old and still ain't married. They ain't a man around here who wants to put up with the kind of smart-mouthed backtalk and sassin' you put out. You oughta been settled down by now, but look at you today, still without even as much as a boyfriend, much less a serious beau. You ain't doin' nothin' but makin' things harder for yourself, that's what you're doin', exactly like your daddy says. As sure as the world, girl, you're headed for a fall!"

"Well, if I do 'fall,' whatever in hell that means," Mock screamed back at her well-intentioned but desperately exasperated parents, "it'll be me that does the fallin', won't it! It won't be you two, so why in hell do you have to bitch about every damned thing I want to do? All I hope is that if I do fall, I fall as far the hell away from this place as possible. Why can't you two leave me alone, mind your own business, and let me live my life!"

"You may not give a damn what people around here are sayin' and thinkin' about you or about our family, but we do!" her father thundered back. "We gotta live here, and you know as well as we do that nobody around here does anything without ever body else knowin' everything there is to know about it. If you're livin' under my roof and eatin' my food, by God, you're damned well gonna do like I say!"

"Like hell I do, and like hell I will!" Mock screamed back. Then she turned the knob, threw open the door, and angrily stormed out into the dusk. She was far past caring what her parents or others thought about anything. It really did not matter how anyone else looked at her. She was determined to leave the damned place as soon as she could make it happen.

"Just you try and stop me," she threatened, as the door slammed shut behind her, leaving her parents, as she had on many other occasions, wringing their hands, knowing — just as well as their daughter did — that there was not a single thing they could do to hold her back. Any possibility of physical restraint had long been off the table.

They had gone down this same virulently argumentative road with one another so often in recent years that the three of them had become word-weary and exasperated. Unable to help themselves, each one of them had said things that could not be taken back or forgotten, much less forgiven. It was too late for that. Their individual breaking points had long since been reached, and each one of them had snapped. Under normal circumstances, the relationships between family members meant loving each other forever, but they had crossed a threshold from which going back was no longer an option. Each one of them was about to break, and all three of them knew it. It was no longer a matter of if; it had become a matter of when!

THE INDIAN
TERRITORY BURNHAMS

ORDINARILY, LITTLE WOULD be known about the day-to-day life experiences of a now long-deceased Creek Indian girl who was born in 1862 out in the Oklahoma Indian Territory, but in Etta "Mock" Burnham's case two sources of information make her story somewhat of an exception. One of those sources is a regional newspaper article that, among other things, highlighted a few of the many misadventures of her husband Early Tiger. He had a reputation for being a locally notorious character before he died in the early 1900s. The other source was a set of collected recollections of her and her husband handed down via word-of-mouth by the children and grandchildren of folks who were around before the two of them died. Other than these two sources, and the basic data that was available through Creek Indian roll sheets and allotment records, no other information about the girl's existence could be found.

That an article including a sketch of her husband's disreputable life ever appeared in print is nothing short of amazing. since it had been impossible to say anything worthwhile or positive about the man while he was alive. Except for this one write-up, no other information about him was available, nothing more than the same basic data that was available for Mock through

Creek Indian roll sheets and allotment records.

Similarly, only the most basic level of anecdotal information was available to describe Early and Mock's relationship while they were married. In their case, the lack of information was due as much as anything to the private and nearly totally obscure lives they lived after they went off on their own as a couple. They were isolated by choice, even among the residents of what most any contemporary observer would have described as an isolated Creek Indian community.

Mock lived with her parents Andy and Ruby Burnham in a home located within the borders of the geographical area that in their day defined the independent and self-governing Creek Nation of the Territory. The little settlement they lived in was situated in the portion of the Nation that upon statehood in November of 1907 was defined as McIntosh County. Later, in 1918, political jurisdiction over the town was transferred to Okmulgee County.

The settlement had a population of around 250 souls, and the majority of those who lived therein and as well as in the surrounding countryside were legal citizens of the Creek Nation. Some non-Creeks lived there as well. Stationed among the Creeks, for example, were a U. S. Army sergeant who commanded a small detachment of troops who were there on temporary duty out of Fort Sill, the United States Army fort that had military jurisdiction over their region of the Territory. The detachment was there to deal with any problems that the Creeks, who were essentially a self-governing people, were not jurisdictionally authorized or otherwise properly prepared to handle for themselves.

Also living in or around the community were an influential and therefore to most of the legal Creeks residents an aggravatingly intrusive smattering of white and black residents who were well known to be illegal settlers. At the time, land in the Territory was not open for legal ownership by outsiders, but they were there, nevertheless. Although they were tolerated by the Creeks, many resented them in equal measure.

In addition to the residents who have been identified, there lived two more individuals who were highly influential and widely recognized as local authority figures, mostly due to the kind of work they did on behalf of the Creeks and as well as other residents of the region. The two people were a couple, each one of them a combination schoolteacher and missionary evangelist. They were Sunday school teachers as well.

The settlement all these folks lived in was so small that it appeared on maps of that part of the Territory only as a populated place, a designation it held for many years. It was not graced with named legal status until April 13, 1906, when a group of local leaders submitted a Petition of Incorporation to officially designate it as the named townsite of Hoffman. This happened over a year before Oklahoma was admitted as a state of the Union on November 16, 1907. Upon statehood, Hoffman ended up within a six-square-mile block of land that was defined as McDaniel Township, but for the remainder this story it will be referred to as the community or the town or, as it was initially described, a populated place.

In the years before incorporation, as well as for years thereafter, the population of the settlement was made up of no more than the gaggle of residents who have been described. Nearly every one of them spent the greater part of daily life engaged in an unending struggle to get by in their extremely remote location, which was widely looked upon back then as not only isolated but as an undesirable wilderness. It was not easy to get to, nor was it an easy place to make a decent living.

The problem that consumed Andy and Ruby Burnham's daily lives out in their Indian Territory remoteness was neither unusual nor of any great historical significance, although it might as well have been, in view of how greatly it had disrupted their mundane existence. On top of the struggles of daily living, they were caught up in a predicament as ordinary as toast and as old as the hills. Their problem was that they had discovered how hopelessly unequal they had been to the task of properly raising their child through adolescence, up to young adulthood, and finally getting her out on her own.

More pointedly, Mock had always been far too shamelessly rebellious for them to control. As far as they were concerned, inexplicably intransigent behavior on her part had proven again and again that she was far more troubled than any other young girl in the general area. Despite long years of doing their level best to guide her down a straight and narrow path, they had become too worn down and bedraggled to continue doing what they knew without question needed to be done. Their well-meant but often unintentionally too heavy-handed past efforts to steer her in a positive direction had not produced the kind of results that they, especially Andy, had expected.

Living in a household that had been in an uproar for as long as they could remember had worn all three of them down to a nub, and the tension of their constant conflict had exacted an overwhelmingly heavy toll. Unhappily, things were not getting any better. Their constant embroilment in a vicious cycle of argument after argument had created a miserable existence for them, to the extent of none of them being able to envision any way of escaping its pull. As far as the principals were concerned, their situation was hopeless.

No family is exempt from the possibility of becoming caught up in the kind of drama that enveloped the Burnhams, no matter what ethnic, racial, religious makeup is under examination. It could happen to any family, anywhere. Dealing with young people, especially during and immediately after their teenage years, can become an insurmountable task for any set of parents. For some couples, no matter how conscientiously they go about performing their filial duties, the regrettable verity remains that the process of raising a youngster to adulthood does not always play out according to the book. In some cases, the parental role can become an absolute nightmare, and this is exactly what happened to Andy and Ruby Burnham.

As husband and wife, Andy and Ruby had been as conscious of the difficulties and realities of their situation as any set of parents in their civic setting. They had the same level of experience, and they had been as dutiful in terms of performing the parental role as any other couple they knew. For that matter, they had been even more committed to performing their role than others. Sadly, though, when it came to rearing their daughter, due diligence had not been nearly enough. Their limited knowledge and skills left them unable to contend with their unfailingly obstinate youngster. As far as they were concerned, they had failed miserably. Dealing with Mock had gradually worn them down, and no mishmash of truisms about effective parenting could overcome that blunt and brutal reality.

The only thing their wretched experience in child rearing had made abundantly clear to them was that parents can take only so much before they break, and that point, as far as they were concerned, was right before their eyes. It was, in their view, only a matter of how and when.

ETTA JANE "MOCK" BURNHAM

ETTA JANE "MOCK" BURNHAM grew to young adulthood in what for her had been miserably close, wretchedly uncomfortable proximity to her fundamentalist, socially ultraconservative parents. They lived in a modest wood framed home that was located way out in the remote section of the Territory that has previously been described. The Burnham residence had seen its better days, but it was still one of the better-kept places in their dirt-poor rural community.

Her parents were proud people, which meant that keeping up appearances meant a great deal to them. Like most of their neighbors, they did not have a whole lot, at least not in material terms. Except for a little better than average decorative attention and attentive routine upkeep, their place was essentially the same as other places scattered around and about them. They really hadn't done a great deal to improve the exterior esthetics of their little place, but the few special steps they had taken did serve notice of some degree of extra sobriety and orderliness on their part as homeowners.

Their home, for example, was among the few in the settlement that was coated in white paint and surrounded by a picket fence of the same color. Although the paint was faded, it still made their place stand out in an area where most homes were lathed in bare and weathered boards. These two distinguishing features, when combined with the flowers they had planted in rows on both sides of the walk leading up to their front porch and their small but well-tended side garden, were more than enough to indicate greater than average pride of place.

The Burnhams were not wealthy or prominent, but they valued their place within their community. Maintaining the respect and goodwill of their neighbors meant a great deal to them, which was why they had endeavored over the years to build up their reputation as a proper, responsible couple. Their diligent efforts, as far as they were concerned, had paid off handsomely, in that most of their neighbors did consider them to be honorable and upright members of their Creek Indian society. That, as far as the two of them were concerned, was exactly how they wanted things to stay.

Due to their pride of place and desire for social approbation, Andy and Ruby were appalled by the turmoil that had been taking place in their formerly stolid and peaceful home. The highly vocal series of arguments that were open-ended between themselves and Mock made it painfully obvious to their neighbors that conditions in their household were far more miserable than exterior appearances suggested.

They were so profoundly disturbed by the depth by which their stature had fallen that they had concluded that something had to be done to stop the profound embarrassment. They could no longer abide the kind of behavior their daughter had been subjecting them to on a regular basis. For them, it was shameful to stand by and watch as the communal standing they had so diligently cultivated over the years was slowly dismantled. They could no longer tolerate it.

Their home was no longer a happy place, and it had not been one for way too many years. From their perspective, their own daughter had turned their household into a subject of local gossip, ridicule, and, worse still, the object of outright pity. As far as they were concerned, it had to stop, one way or another.

In this their most recent argument, they wanted to do whatever could be done to steer Mock away from a yet another setting that would not be good for her. They believed they were intervening in the same way responsible parents anywhere would have, faced with the same combination of circumstances. There was no way that going alone to a damned drunken stomp was a good thing for her to do, not under any set of circumstance. It was as clear as a bell to them, so they could not understand why in hell their silly girl would not do as she was told. It was clear that she was going to ignore them yet again this time around, as was so commonly the case, and that, like always, their good intentions would come to naught.

Damn it all, they though to themselves: Yet another interaction begun in the sparsely furnished living room of their modest home between themselves and their unrepentantly disobedient daughter had disintegrated into a gut-churningly bitter verbal battle. Why, they wondered, did their talk always go that way? There was nothing unusual about their interaction having gone the way it did; it had happened again and again, in precisely the same way. They knew in their hearts that their daughter was totally out of control.

Although Mock was 20 years-old, she still lived under their roof. Inexplicably to Andy, her behavior had grown even worse than it had been when she was younger. Recollections of an altercation she'd had a few years back with their neighbor's daughter Nadine Blackwell flashed through his mind. The conflagration that had come to mind was only one in a string of many others of its kind, but it was one that had turned out to be as mortifying as it was aggravating.

It started one afternoon when Mock happened to notice Nadine teasing and joking and otherwise coming on way too cozily to a young man by the name of Chuff Robertson, the son of yet another neighbor, as the two of them stood with a group of young singles in front of the mercantile store that housed the post office.

Several of their mutual friends could not help but observe that something out of the ordinary seemed to be going on between Chuff and Nadine, some unascertainable something that caused them to sneak occasional furtive glances in Mock's direction as well, all for the sake of gauging how she might react. They knew Mock thought Chuff was partial to her, although the two of them had established no, so to speak, officially exclusive relationship.

Mock most definitely noticed what was taking place, but she pretended that she had not. She had also noted and fully understood exactly what the other girls were thinking. Nadine and Chuff's interest in one another was apparent to everyone but Nadine and Chuff, who were temporarily oblivious to how they were coming across. The other girls knew that Mock did not like what she saw.

Despite knowing what the other girls were thinking, Mock did not respond in the heat of the moment to the way Nadine was behaving, nor did she display any obvious sign of jealousy or anger. Instead, she pointedly continued doing whatever it was that she had gone to the mercantile store to do, holding herself in check until later. She knew Chuff would have to leave for work before long, and that soon afterwards all the girls, including herself, would head for home for the evening, each going their separate ways.

After Chuff departed as expected a little while later, the girls started saying their goodbyes to one another before going their separate ways toward home. Mock said in passing to Nadine and several other girls that she wanted to walk for a little while before they all went home. She asked if Nadine would like to walk along with them.

In the interest of smoothing over any possible misunderstanding Mock might have locked in on due to her interaction with Chuff, Nadine immediately agreed.

As they walked toward the bend, Nadine volunteered, "Chuff and I were only talking. There's really nothing to speak of between us."

The other girls, though, including Mock, knew

without asking that their conversation had been something more than that, although none of them could have said exactly how much more. That, of course, should have been a private matter, something solely between Nadine and Chuff.

"Don't worry about it," Mock responded, adding, "he isn't a boyfriend, so I don't have any special hold on him."

"Great," Nadine said, "because I don't want you to get the wrong idea. Like I said, we were only talking."

"No problem," Mock replied, within earshot of the other girls, who both Mock and Nadine had known since they were kids and considered mutual friends. She said to the others, "Why don't all of you stop by the bend so we can smoke a while before we go on home? I want to tell Nadine what I know about Chuff. I've learned a few things about him she certainly might want to know."

"Sounds good to me," Nadine readily agreed. She felt relieved that Mock seemed to be taking the situation better than she feared would be the case.

The other girls were not fooled by Mock's congeniality. They realized right away that Mock might not be nearly as okay with what had happened as she let on.

The bend was a small but semiprivate location within one of the folds of a slow flowing creek, which right through the middle of town. Along its meandering path between and past various homes in the community, small pools had been created at a few of the multiple turns. Aside one of the larger bends, brush and small trees had grown up in such a way as to create a private, sheltered spot. It was a sandy beach-like location where it was possible for a small group to congregate in relative privacy, Despite its proximity to the middle of town. In the normal course of things, people walked by the spot regularly, but those who were within it were too concealed to be seen.

The bend was such a pleasant and convenient place to stop off at for a few private moments that it was frequented by young people as well as mature adults, with the adults stopping there for pretty much the same reasons as the young folks. Typically, they drank or smoked or carried on in ways they would not have out in the open. The girls, for example, stopped off there whenever they could, usually to sneak in an illicit smoke.

Mock, Nadine, and the other girls soon arrived at the sheltered clearing. They stood around, talking to one another, Mock faced Nadine with her hands out. In one hand was a hand-rolled cigarette that she offered to Nadine. While Nadine was looking down at the cigarette, Mock suddenly dropped the smoke and without warning, slapped Nadine across the face as forcefully as she could. At that point, the two girls tore into one another with a vengeance, and the result was an absolute blowout. The other girls immediately knew it was going to be a momentous brawl, one that would be remembered for a long time thereafter.

The last thing Nadine wanted was to take part in a physical confrontation, but she had no choice but to do her level best to put up a defense. Because Mock was stronger, she immediately got the better of things, as she had known all along would be the case. Mock was fully aware of her strengths and weaknesses, relative to the other girls.

As the other girls watched, Mock got Nadine flat on her back, set astride her, and started slapping her as often and as hard as she could manage, occasionally jerking out as much hair as she could get a hold on. Nadine wailed all the while, pleading for Mock to stop. Mock didn't stop, though; she continued to beat on Nadine until the other girls interceded and made her stop. If they had not done so, there was no telling how long the beating would have gone on.

Shaken and in tears upon her release, Nadine ran straight home and told her parents what had happened. Her parents, in turn, went directly to Andy and Ruby's front door. They stood on the doorstep as angry as any set of parents would have been under the same circumstance. They raised holy hell over how Mock had beaten their daughter, demanding that something be done about it. "Mock, they said, "damned well deserves to be punished!"

At first, Andy and Ruby, rose to their daughter's defense, as might be expected. They figured that if a fight had broken out between two girls, then each one of them must have been partially responsible for it having happened. For once, they hoped, Mock might not be solely at fault.

They were forced to relent, however, as soon as a full account of the incident was made clear to them.

From her condition, it was obvious that Nadine had not been the aggressor and that the encounter had really been more of a beating than a true fight among equals. With so many witnesses, there was no doubt at all about what had happened. In the end, Andy and Ruby had no choice but to admit that Mock had caused the whole shameful brouhaha.

They had no choice but to apologize profusely to Nadine's parents, and then to Nadine on Mock's behalf. They said they would do what they could to make Mock apologize as well. When she would not, they apologized yet again on her behalf, saying that that kind of thing would never happen again and promising that she would be appropriately punished.

Punishing Mock by whipping her with a switch had not done one whit of good; she still refused to relent. Andy remembered as clear as day how she reacted, recalling that Mock could not have been any more unrepentant if she had tried. What the hell is wrong with the girl, he thought to himself afterwards. Now, here he was, many years after the shameful incident, still wondering the same damned thing.

What stood out more than anything to the girls who witnessed the outright beating was that after the event Mock never again had anything to speak of to do with Chuff, the boy the brawl had been about. Why not? they wondered, if she was as jealous as it had appeared. Not a one of them could figure it out. Why all the ruckus, they wondered, if she wasn't interested in the guy? Mock, to their amazement, seemed perfectly okay with the way things turned out, since Nadine never had much more to do with Chuff, either.

"There had to be some sort of message or meaning associated with what we witnessed," one of the girls said to another, but not a one of them could figure out or even have begun to explain what it might have been. All they could conclude from the incident was how unwise it was to get crosswise with Mock, since there was no doubt that something wrong in her head, in one indiscernible way or another. The overridingly important lesson each one of them took away from having witnessed the fight was that they ought to tread lightly when they were around Etta Jane "Mock" Burnham.

Any deference she was able to garner from her peers was pleasing to Mock, if for no other reason than that it made her stand out and thus feel better about herself among them. Being considered a person apart was exactly what she was after, since the last thing she wanted was to be visualized as being like anyone else who lived in the community she loathed.

What Mock saw as respectful deference on the part of the other girls was based far more on fearful caution than any level of genuine esteem for her. Even if she had known their true feeling it wouldn't have mattered to her. In her mind, deference required being different, and being different, as far as she was concerned, meant being better. Being looked upon in that light meant more to her than anything else, including her relationship with Chuff Robertson.

Not a one of her friends could have explained the

weird relation that existed between themselves and Mock, nor could Mock have explained it herself. The difference hovered between them, even though not a one of them could have described it.

*****

TO ANDY AND RUBY, their family situation had grown more humiliating with every year that passed, especially since in a community like theirs everybody knew everybody and nothing about anybody was ever fully confidential. They knew that their neighbors were fully aware of what had been going on within their home, and this mortified them to no end. Thinking about how low they had fallen in the esteem of friends and neighbors left them feeling heartsick. They loved their wayward daughter, but their inability to control her had driven them to the point of despair.

No matter how upset they were, Andy and Ruby knew all too well that they were powerless to do anything more than watch as Mock angrily grasped the knob of the door in their home that opened into the outside world and slammed it shut against them. In their eyes, their daughter was barging straight out into a world full of more outright evil than any girl of her age and experience could possibly imagine. Although they were as angry with her as it was possible for a set of parents to be, even that was not enough to keep the darkest thoughts about the many God-awful things that could happen to her at bay. Their minds were filled with dread. Because they were her parents, no matter how bad relations between them became, they still loved her.

Despite their anguish, all Andy and Ruby were able to do after their argument with Mock on the early evening of the day of the stomp was sit together in the living room of their tiny home, wringing their hands over what might happen that later that night. Occasionally, one, then the other, would rise and peer gloomily out the front window. They commiserated over the agonies of their relationship with Mock, too baffled by her behavior to come up with any explanation for how or why things between them had gone so far off the rails.

After she stormed away from home and tore off in the direction of the rally point for the dance, they ended up doing what they always did in the wake of one of their blowouts: They lamented to one another, asking each other repeatedly, "How in the hell could we have gone so wrong with our girl?"

In truth, Andy and Ruby had long since concluded that nothing they had done or failed to do had brought about the level of toxicity that existed between themselves and Mock. It was not their fault, they had decided. The responsibility was hers, not theirs, since she seemed to want things between them to be the way they were when they most definitely did not. It was the way she was, even if it made no sense at all. They could not think of a single thing that could be done to turn the situation around. They had tried everything. Even a blind man, they believed, could see that Mock was out of control. In the end, their thoughts always gravitated right back to the same conclusion: they most definitely did not deserve the trash their daughter routinely dished out to them, and that's all there was to it.

Worn down by frustration and anger, they ended up right where they always did in the aftermath of an argument with their daughter: staring blankly at one another, worried sick by thoughts of the wide range of disasters that might befall a child, especially a wayward daughter, whose behavior was no longer subject to parental or any other form of control. The possibilities seemed endless, and the outcome of every one of those possibilities could, as far as they were concerned, be even more depressingly awful than the one before. They eventually ended up so upset that they could not think about much of anything else.

Unlike Mock, Andy and Ruby were acutely aware of the Territory of their day and time most definitely being a rough and dangerous place. Nobody had to remind them that there were people living around them who had well deserved reputations for being so brutal towards others as to be senseless in the extreme. For readily understandable reasons, there was no wonder why they were worried sick over what might happen to an angry daughter who stormed away from home, intent on spending a night out alone at what they knew could turn into another of those damnable drunken stomps.

MOCK'S ANGRY DEPARTURE
FOR THE STOMP

FROM THE MOMENT she departed from home on the evening of the dance, it would have been clear to any dispassionate observer that Mock did not give more than a whit of thought to any of Andy and Ruby's fears about what might happen to her later that night. Her mind was operating without any semblance of rational thought. She was far too angry for that.

Just as she had threatened to do, she barged straight out toward the rally point over at Harley Wilson's barn. She was intent on taking advantage of the drayman's for-a-pittance wagon ride over to the stomp grounds out past the nearby small town of Hitchita. Come hell or high water, she swore to herself, I'm going to go to that damned stomp, whether my parents want me to or not.

She knew as well as her parents that getting to the dance by means of Wilson's conveyance was her only option, since there was no other form of transportation that she could afford and would want to utilize. She had known without asking that her father would not have let her use their own horse and wagon that evening. Even if he had been willing to let her use their rig, all three of them knew that the last thing any of them wanted was for her to have to worry about traveling back home alone late at night after the dance.

Beyond its low cost, the major advantage of traveling to the stomp grounds on the hay strewn bed of Wilson's freight wagon was that his team could be depended on to get passengers safely back to his barn, even if they returned late at night. It was well known in the surrounding area how through the years his old draft horses had been conditioned via force of habit to do exactly that. Getting home was so ingrained in the team that they could be relied upon to get back to their stall, even if every person on board — including the driver, Harley himself — was stumbling drunk or, for that matter, passed out fully before or shortly after they departed from the stomp site. It was typical of Harley, for one, to do exactly that.

Anyone who had witnessed the all-out row that took place earlier that evening between Mock and her parents would have noted after no more than a few minutes of reflection that she was too unstable and immature to understand what might happen out at the social gathering she was about to get herself into. In her own eyes, she was as tough as nails, fully self-reliant, and ready to take on all comers, when she was not even close to being worldly enough to appreciate the potential ramifications of what she had decided to do. She was too inexperienced to know that she was about to place herself in a position that could quickly become a lot more threatening than she would be able to handle.

Among the many points her parents had reminded her of earlier in the evening — the only one Mock fully appreciated — was what they had said about the nature of their small community. She could not have agreed more with their point that in their remote corner of the world, everyone truly did know everybody else's business. She knew exactly what they hoped she would not do, which was for her to damage their image in the community even more than she already had. People were gossiping enough about them as it was. To Mock, though, always having to worry about making that kind of mistake was one more vivid example of what was so awful about where they lived. She regularly referred to it as the damned little rat hole of a town they lived in.

To hell with all of them, she swore to herself under her breath. She discounted not only her parents' admonitions but also the moral standards of respectable members of the community, not to mention ordinary common sense. She felt so stifled by her environment — especially when it came to strictures imposed by her parents, relatives, and neighbors — that she was too disgusted to care one way or the other what any of them thought about her or about anything else.

Mock knew her parents had wished for all the world that they could have held her back from going out that night, but she also knew that neither one of them would have dared an attempt to physically restrain her. They knew they could not. She knew she was a very sturdy girl, way too much more of a girl than either one of them could handle, considering how their health had deteriorated in recent years.

Physical and mental toughness were two attributes Mock very much wanted people to associate with her. She felt she had to be seen in those ways, for no reason other than to be able to breathe freely. Because she visualized herself to be a rough-and-tumble sort of girl, over the past few years she had devoted a great deal of effort to making sure others saw her that way as well. She wanted to come across as blunt, bluff, and haughty, so she had done her best to carry herself accordingly.

Those who truly knew her, particularly acquaintances of her own age, would not have hesitated to point out that she was always more aggressive than made any sense. In addition, they thought her overall behavior was far more risqué than any young woman ought to display, there or anywhere else. Her female peers knew, for example, that she never hesitated to banter in passing with the older guy many residents of their town derisively referred to (always behind his back) as "Crazy Early," when they would never even have considered doing such a thing themselves. Egging on or in any way encouraging a guy like that was, as far as they were concerned, behavior beyond the pale.

Mock was not an unattractive young woman, although she was more average looking than an out-and-out beauty. Like a good number of her tribal counterparts, she was a just a little overweight, but she was raw-boned, rugged, and physically fit, on top of being a few inches taller than average. She behaved the way she did because she had convinced herself that it was essential for people to think of her as a girl who could take care of herself, come what may. To her, it was yet another way of distinguishing herself among her peers.

She imagined her passing interactions with Early Tiger to be nothing more than idle chatter that occasionally did get a little too raw at times, but most of the young women who observed them together could see that it came across to him as something more than that. They thought he saw their interaction as more of an invitation than she intended, but when one of them said so, Mock's response was to laugh them off. Her peers, thought, did not take her behavior so lightly.

It was not surprising that girls of her own age saw Mock's interaction with Crazy Early in a negative light, especially since every one of them did whatever they could to avoid striking up any sort of relationship with him at all, not even the casual kind of association Mock had with him. They wanted nothing to do with the man at all — not in any way, shape, or form. Eligible males in the area reacted in pretty much the same way, in that they wanted nothing to do with Early, either. After they heard that Early was somewhat taken by Mock, they shied away from her from that point forward. Because she had no real interest in Early at all, Mock knew nothing about any of this.

Despite these undercurrents, no one ever seriously cautioned Mock about the way she interacted with Early, mainly because she was not only taller than most of her acquaintances but also young and healthy and strong.   Her acquaintances, like her parents, had known for ages that she was stepping out of bounds and taking way too many chances, although they never openly said so. Because they knew how argumentative and aggressive Mock could become, they avoided saying anything that might cross her. They knew she would not hesitate to tear into them if they made any effort to contradict or otherwise go against her. Mock's behavior puzzled every person who knew her, and, for reasons even she could not have explained or justified, she seemed to like it that way.

Throughout her childhood Mock's parents had tried their best to lay down reasonable rules for her to live by, but nothing they tried had worked. Headstrong to a fault from her earliest years, she had always been one to go her own way and to keep her own counsel. She had made her own rules for as long as anyone could remember. Because she had been the same way since she was a young girl, the whole community knew exactly what she was like. Then, right after she turned thirteen, sexual promiscuity became a new part of what was already a volatile mix and led to changes that made her bad attitude worse than ever.

EARLY "HAWK" TIGER

AT AROUND THE SAME HOUR that Mock defiantly slammed the door of her family home and tore off into the evening, another resident of the community was also preparing to attend the stomp. Those who ran with the man called him "Hawk," but others, always behind his back, referred to him as "Crazy Early." His approach to preparing for the evening was nothing like hers; in fact, it was night-and-day different. Still and all, it would be right on the money to say that both of their approaches to preparing for the evening out were equally ill advised, in that both were rife with possibilities for getting them into trouble, only in different ways.

No reasonable person would describe departing from home in a blind rage after yet another senselessly caustic argument with her parents a good start for an evening out on the town, but Mock had done exactly that. And almost anyone who witnessed it would have described Early's method of gearing up for the evening as even more unwise than Mock's.

Early's preparation began with tipping back shots of whiskey until he got to feeling light-headed and happy, and it ended when he got to the point of feeling that he was up to taking on whatever situations might arise later that night. Come what may, he wanted to be ready for any situation, since, in his case, something usually did come up.

Becoming aggressive after beginning to drink was normal behavior for Early, and it was in no way uncommon for him to end up looking for a fight whenever he got drunk. His proclivity for drunkenness had gotten him into all kinds of trouble in past years, but he was nevertheless nearly always drunk. Within the community, it had been clear for some time that Early Tiger had become his own worst enemy.

Although Early wanted to be mentally prepared for any anything that might come up that night at the dance, he was in no way worried about the likelihood of his own drunkenness getting him into trouble. He didn't give it a thought. For him, besottedness was a norm, not an aberration. He stayed drunk pretty much whenever he could afford to do so. His only real concern before striking out for the evening had to do with being sure he avoided running into his drinking buddy Dub, to whom he owned a share of the proceeds from the sale of some sacks of pecans the two of them had stolen and that he was supposed to have sold for their mutual benefit. Dub was due half of the proceeds, but, having drunk up all the money, Early knew he could not pay up. He knew for damned sure that Dub was not going to like it.

In a way, Mock and Early were two peas in a pod, in that the two of them shared an appallingly senseless tendency to double down on the same kind of behavior that had gotten them into trouble in the past. Seemingly unable to learn from their mistakes, their excursions out nearly always began with another round of the same kind of foolishness that has been described. Neither one of them ever seemed to realize that the best way to stay out of trouble was to avoid messing up their minds before walking out of their own homes.

They lived their daily lives on totally different planes, but one notable behavioral trait Mock and Early had in common was that it was typical of them to depart in a foul mood whenever they headed out for another of what either one of them would have unhesitatingly described as a night of fun. By the time they linked up with other people, their negative attitudes usually stood out like red flags and as would be expected one thing always seemed to lead to another.

What all this meant on a practical level is that the evening of the dance began for them on the same kind of sour note that many other outings had for them in recent years. She was as mad as hell and in a rotten state of mind even before she raged away from her parents' home, and he was almost fully drunk and already spoiling for a fight even before stepping over the threshold of the grungy little place on the outskirts of town that was his home. Angry at the world for their own inexplicable reasons, they had chips on their shoulders before they closed their doors behind them.

As far as the two of them were concerned, it was never their own fault that so many interactions with others ended up on a sorry note. She blamed her parents for her problems; he blamed society at large. They were both wrong, in that they were their own worst enemies. The one unequivocal observation even a blind man would have made about each of them before they left home on the night of the ill-fated stomp was that, in view of their respective states of mind, they were likely to draw trouble like a magnet.

This was true for them both, but it was clearly much more so for a man who had earned a reputation bad enough for most everyone to refer to him as Crazy Early. It was easy to see that his attitude of mind was a recipe for causing a problem of one kind or another, if not an outright disaster.

ANGST,
HONESTLY COME BY?

WAS IT HONESTLY come-by angst that turned Early Tiger into the angry and broken-down man he became over the years, or were his many problems caused by more prosaic human weaknesses? There is no definitive answer for this question. Sophisticated analysis or insightful explanation of his mental issues were not available in his remote neck of the woods while he was alive. Therefore, there will never be a clear-cut answer to this most basic of questions about this troubled man.

As far as residents of the community were concerned, Early Tiger bumped up against the law as often as he did because he was way more than half-crazy. That, in their view, was why he went around halfcocked as often as he did. The most appropriate way to deal with him, locals would have unhesitatingly asserted, was to throw his ass in jail and leave him to seethe until the attitude adjustment he was so obviously in need of finally took place.

For the most part, conscious thought about this troubled man's condition never went much deeper than that, which is why so much of Early's life flew by while he was behind bars. Nobody could envision any better way of dealing with him.

Despite the majority public opinion, Early Tiger and other troubled Indian men like him had their apologists, no matter how mindless or inexplicably self-destructive the predicaments they got themselves into happened to be. Their defenders were quick to assert how subliminal factors must have had at least some role — perhaps even a major role — in producing the inner turmoil by which hapless men like them were tormented. Early, viewed from this perspective, was most certainly further gone than most.

The defense put forth on Early's behalf was that he, like so many other Indian men of his period, was disturbed in ways that he could not comprehend and, therefore, could not be overtly controlled. His clashes with authority figures, for example, ought to be considered symptomatic of fundamental realities he had to live with, whether he knew it or not. Adjudication of any offenses he committed, folks who saw things this way contended, had to be conducted with this thought in mind, if for no reason than for the sake of basic fairness. At the very least, due consideration of the special difficulties Indian men like him had to cope with ought to mitigate the severity of any punishment meted for their crossings of societal lines. In other words, "Give him a break; the man has a lot of problems."

Regrettably, though, for Early as well as for other Indian men of his period, leniency was not a highly ranked consideration when it came to the administration of justice in the Territory, not for his kind or for anyone else. Punishment tended to be swift and harsh, especially for Indian men who got too far out of control. People got sick of seeing and hearing about the kinds of crimes they committed and the sort of behavior they exhibited in public, which included public intoxication, intimidation, and fighting, as well as serious crimes such as stealing, beating, and murdering. Public sentiment favored authorities who were willing to throw the book at them.

In most cases, leniency was not the first public reaction in situations like those Early tended to get himself into, any more than it was a highly valued trait among the law enforcement officials of his vicinity. Among law enforcement officers, head-bangers were far more common in the ranks than do-gooders. For this reason, it would be fair to say that in his setting it was risky business for Indian men or, for that matter, anyone else to buck too hard against the law. The problem, though, according to Indian defenders was that this happened to be much truer for Indians than for whites.

Despite the outlook that prevailed at the time, there were people around who considered it obvious as well as understandable that boiling inner disquiet within some Indian men would be manifested in the form of such highly visible outward problems as indolence, drunkenness, seething resentment, and, on occasion, seemingly mindless outbursts of anger. Was there any more logical way, the folks who thought this way might have asked, to explain the patently self-destructive behavior that was so common among the Indian men they saw around them?

You would be angry too, these folks would have asserted, if your people had been subjected to — and, for that matter, were still being subjected to — that kind of mistreatment. This, in their view, was a salient reality that had to be kept in mind, especially when it came to the administration of justice. In too many cases, they believed, Indian offenders were subjected to harsher punishment than was truly warranted.

Many whites of the period considered bad behavior on the part of Indian men as additional evidence in support of what they already believed, which was that theirs was a superior race. In their view, any crime that was committed by an indolent, drunken Indian man was intolerable, no matter what may have caused it. Their attitude gave rise to even more bias, prejudice, and outright hostility between the races, during a period when those problems were already too prevalent.

It goes without saying that thoughts and attitudes of this kind could have not been good for anyone, Indian or white. Even more regrettable is that many of the same problems that plagued the Indians of Early's day carried forward through the years, causing whites of later periods to think of them in the same way they did back then.

The concept of inherited angst gained whatever minimal traction it did because it was, in effect, one of the few ways that sympathizers had for crying out against not only how the Creeks as well as other tribes wound up out in Territory in the first place, but also how they were exploited for years thereafter. Their story was tragic enough to elicit the sympathy on the part of fair-minded people back when it was happening, and the same sentiment has existed from that point forward. When historical facts are duly considered, it becomes a lot easier to appreciate why some consider the concept of inherited angst to be an understandable way of thinking.

How the Creeks wound up in the Indian Territory is one of the grimmest of grim stories, in that it is about how a stronger power stomped down a weaker one and then expropriated most everything of value they had. The Creeks certainly did not volunteer for what happened to them, that's for sure.

HANDED-DOWN BITTERNESS

DURING THE 1830S AND 1840S, Early's parents along with other members of their tribe, the Creeks, were removed from their homes in the southeastern part of the United States and forcibly relocated in the remote Oklahoma Indian Territory. They did not welcome the move; it was forced upon them.

The relocation of most members of their tribe was completed through a series of operations much like those that have been collectively described as the Cherokees' Trail of Tears. Group after group was escorted on their way, until the government had dealt with as many members of the tribe as could be rounded up. For many of them, the relocation turned out to be a miserable, humiliating experience.

Not surprisingly, the relocation became an episode some Creeks were never able to forget or to forgive. When it was coupled with other incidences of what Early's predecessors saw as egregious wrongs that had been committed against them, many of them hated whites for the remainder of their lives.

Be that as it may, tribal members were powerless to do much of anything about their predicament. Whether they liked it or not, no choice was open to them but to move out west to the Indian Territory. The result was that for generations thereafter, resentment against white authority was passed down through many Creek fathers to their sons.

Whites coveted the land the Indians lived on in the southeast part of the country, notably in parts of Georgia, Alabama, North Carolina, and Florida. The Creeks and other tribes were relocated to tracts of treaty land that was set aside for them by the federal government. The problem with this fair-sounding relocation plan, as far as most members of the tribes were concerned, was that the location they were involuntarily shipped off to was generally regarded by whites and Indians alike as a highly undesirable and lawless wilderness. Records from the period indicate that if they had had any real choice in the matter, there is little doubt that the greater percentage of Creeks would never have agreed to give up their ancestral land in the southeastern part of our country.

Early Tiger was born on February 15, 1840, shortly after his parents were relocated to the Indian Territory. Tiger was a well- known and highly regarded Creek family surname. While some members of their tribe were financially well off back then, most of them most definitely were not. Early and his folks were among the many who ended up having to live through some lean and difficult years on the land that had been set aside for them. His people hunted, fished, ranched, and farmed to get by, but it was a tough stretch for most of them.

Members of Early's family lived in relative obscurity out in their remote section of the Territory, which means that under ordinary circumstances only the scantest amount of information would be known about any one of them today. More than a minimum is known about Early. It is only because he was involved in a series of incidents of sufficient local notoriety that a written record about him exists. If not for this happenstance occurrence, he would have remained a nearly obscure and nearly anonymous individual, as is the case for most of his tribal counterparts.

The records that do exist for Early indicate that he ended up becoming a bitter, angry, cruel man. His familial nickname, Hawk, is said to have been bestowed on him by his father, who, as the story goes, shortly after his son was born caught sight of a hawk with a broken wing. It was flitting from limb to limb in a grove of trees down in the Deep Fork River bottom, desperately trying to stay out of sight of human observers. Looking back, Hawk seems an odd nickname for a boy whose family surname was Tiger, but it made sense to his father, and, at the time, his opinion was the only one that mattered. There is no way to verify the truth of this account at this late date, but, true or not, He was known to many of his closer contacts by this nickname for the remainder of his life.

If this recollection from Early's young life really did happen as has been described, it was truly owl-like of the hawk to have tried his best to stay out the line of sight of the tribal people of its area, since it might have ended up in a pot had it been spotted. Birds of prey are not good to eat, but it certainly could have happened, since, when Early was a young man, many of the Indians in his neck of the woods were living lean and hungry lives. Large numbers of them, according to the record, depended on government assistance for much of their sustenance.

Creek names and nicknames had fallen somewhat out of use by his father's and Early's time, since white, or, as they were termed, civilized names, had been assumed by a good number of tribe members back when they were living in the Southeast. A good many Indian families had voluntarily adopted white names back when they still lived there. They hoped that doing so might help them get along with their white neighbors and thereby give them a better chance of holding on to their land and basic customs. Some unusual sounding (at least to white ears) names resulted from this voluntary practice. One fellow, for example, because he liked the sound and simplicity of the name Bill, renamed himself Bill Bill.

Early, in other words, may not have become Early "Hawk" Tiger, a citizen of the Creek Nation of the Oklahoma Indian Territory, through traditional native naming practices, but through his grandparents or parents having voluntarily renamed themselves. Alternatively, they may have voluntarily parted with their Creek names after having "white" ones suggested for them by authorities after they arrived in the Territory. Again, though, no matter how he came to be nicknamed Hawk, some of his closer associates referred to him by that way for the remainder of his life. He had other nicknames as well, most of them not nearly as ennobling as Hawk.

Early's childhood and youth were lived out during trouble filled years in the Territory, during a period that was a challenge for most members of any one of the tribes. Most of the people he grew up around were the offspring of other Indians who had been relocated to the Territory after the expropriation of their land in the eastern part of the country for white settlement. Because resentment over this had remained a sore spot from that point forward, this historical verity could at least partially explain how he came by at least some of the angst by which he was bedeviled as well as why he grew up to be such a troubled and bitter person. Up to the present day, there still are Indians who do not have much of anything good to say about whites or the federal government.

Yet another reality that may have kept Early stirred up during his formative years could been the internecine conflict that had been taking place among the Indians themselves. For various reasons, there was a harmful level of it.

Many differences existed, for example, between the so-called "wild" Indians of the Territory — members of tribes that were native to the area — and members of tribes resettled there from other parts of the country. They had been used to traveling freely throughout the region, but, after other tribes were relocated there, they no longer could come and go as they pleased. For example, only a few years before, the land that was set aside for the Creeks had been the "wild" Indians' exclusive domain. Broadly speaking, the tribes that lived in the Territory while Early was growing up were divisible into these broad groups, and the two groups did not always see eye to eye with one another.

Another fundamental problem among Indians in general was that members of the native or wild tribes were not as advanced in terms of being able to interact with whites or other Indians as were members of the tribes that had been relocated from the East. In addition, the tribes had different languages and cultural traditions that made it difficult for them to communicate and cooperate with each other. Problems caused by these differences combined to increase the number of misunderstandings that came up between these two broad Indian subgroups.

Not much is said about it today, but there were class distinctions as well that existed between and among the native and eastern tribes. Many of the native Indians were more primitive — or, as people would have put it back then — "wilder" than some of the relatively better educated and more politically aware Indians of tribes that had been removed to the Territory from eastern states. For example, many of the native Indians were, for the most part, totally uneducated and still living primitive lives, while some of the resettled eastern Indians could read and write.

In addition, some of the eastern Indians who were moved out west had enough personal wealth to be able to build good homes and acquire various other kinds of valuable personal property, and some of them were even prosperous enough to own slaves. These differences in relative wealth and prosperity led to additional inter-tribal problems.

Sadly, most of the resettled Indians, including members of Early's own family line, were not among those who were blessed with good educations or much material wealth. They were, for intents and purposes, nearly as poor as the wild Indians.

The wild versus civilized distinction was only one of many differences that led to political divisions and splits among the various tribes. It goes without saying that the individual tribes as well as Indians in general would have been better off if they had been able to work together on their collective behalf, but the sad reality was that the many differences between and within the various tribes led to lots of quarrelling. On occasion, these clashes were on par with arguments they had with whites. Many of the various tribes, while they were all Indians, had little understanding or affinity for any of the others. Still, they were forced to live uncomfortably close together, whether they liked it or not, which made bickering common, both between and within the various tribes.

Yet another deep split among the Creeks occurred during the Civil War. One major faction sided with the Union while another, thinking that if the South won it would be more likely to allow their tribe greater latitude and autonomy, sided with the Confederacy. At various locations in or near the Indian Territory during the war years of 1861 through 1865, Creek fighting men engaged in battles to the death with one another, often led by Creek officers on both sides; some held ranks as high as general of the army. The war caused misery among the Creeks, in the same way that it did among and within various states, northern and southern alike.

There is little doubt that Early Tiger grew up among a multitude of terribly embittered people. This truth might explain at some overt or subliminal level, that a portion of the bitterness and ill temper, which got him into so much trouble later in his life, was ignited in this divisive environment.

It is indisputable that Early grew to adulthood during years that were threatening, confusing, and difficult for most Indians of the Territory; times that were more than difficult enough to turn many of them into frustrated human beings. It is not difficult to envision how tribal people who had been overwhelmed and rolled over by outsiders such as soldiers, settlers, missionaries, various government agencies and officials, and others who wound up controlling the most important aspects of their lives might have harbored a high degree of anger and resentment against any of these forces. These were the very forces that combined against them to create the mechanism by which Indians were "contained" and then crowded into ever smaller contiguous areas of land. It is easy to see how this kind of treatment would have alienated them, it the same way that it would have enraged any other group of people.

It is possible that Early Tiger was seriously impacted by inherited angst or, for that matter, even outright anger. That this question would come to mind during any serious contemplation of the kind of man he became is not surprising, since the whole way of life of his people had been turned upside down. It should not be considered totally unexpected that he and others like him might have ended up living lives that would bring them into conflict with white or Creek tribal powers.

In the Creek Indian nation as Early was coming up, chiefs of tribal towns dealt with criminal behavior through their own police forces; although the United States District Court in Fort Smith, Arkansas, the United States Army, or other local white powers were relied upon to deal with certain kinds of law enforcement problems. White authorities got involved in Indian affairs only when there was trouble between Indians and whites, problems between the various tribes, or when other situations cropped up that tribal authorities were not equipped to handle. The United States Army post at Fort Sill up near Oklahoma City had jurisdiction over the area assigned to Early's people.

Even in the face of the common realities Indian people were up against during Early's youth and young adult years, some of the tribes remained uncooperative and unfriendly toward one another. Ongoing antagonisms existed between factions within the various tribes, differences that could not be risen above. The Creeks, for example, were only one of many tribes that were afflicted by this problem, but their internal problems were near-legendary. One result of all the friction among and within the various tribes that existed during Early's younger years was that for him — as well as for many other Indians — it created an even more unsettling, confusing, and demoralizing environment in which to live.

The federal government's approach to helping deal with problems among the Indians of Early's region of the Territory included the funding of missionary societies to help pay for the construction and maintenance of Indian schools and teachers' salaries. The purpose of this effort was to help the Indians pursue a "settled" way of life. In return for this effort, the federal government took for granted that the missionaries would be supportive of various government initiatives, edicts, and programs designed to uplift the tribes. Through this mutually beneficial arrangement, missionary societies effectively became semiofficial agencies of the federal government. Their status gave them a lot of local influence and power.

Despite how the pill was sweetened, only the strength of the forces pitted against them made many Indians swallow their bitter frustration and anger and, ultimately, begin to convert to a white way of life. The wrongs and outright abuses they had to tolerate was substantial, but they had to fall into line whether they wanted to or not.

Indians were exploited, manipulated, and cheated, and not only by white civic authorities. Also preying upon them were illegal settlers, government agents, Indians who were more knowledgeable, and even, in some cases, Christian missionaries. In addition, there are records to prove that some soldiers of the United States Army bullied, mocked, and mistreated them. Some of them, truth be known, hated Indians altogether, due to memories of past depredations.

Although they received some government assistance in the form of yearly annuities and commodities, poverty, homelessness, and near if not outright malnutrition became part and parcel of daily life for many Indians. Those who were not sufficiently adaptable and resourceful often ended up dependent on the federal government, just to get by.

Poverty was common among some of the tribes of Early's region of the Territory, and along with it came its familiar companions: indolence, hopelessness, and alcoholism. The record shows that as the years passed by, many members of many tribes ended up in increasingly desperate straits.

No longer being fully in charge of their own lives turned some Indians into dependents — people who were almost completely reliant on government distributions of meat, seed, flour, corn, blankets, and other commodities to live on. These sad circumstances eventually led to many of them becoming dispirited, to the extent that they began to live dissolute and aimless lives.

Alcoholism, for example, was an affliction that grew among them until it became an absolute curse.

Some of those who fell prey to it evolved into pitiable specimens indeed, and Early Tiger, as the record shows, was one of those who became enslaved by this debilitating addiction.

In summary, little investigation was required to confirm that Early lived during a dreadfully troubling period for Indian people. It was not difficult to confirm that his personal life eventually spiraled completely out of control. His own comments are on file to confirm that he lived a depressingly miserable existence.

Early's situation was probably more descriptive of how life turned out for more Indian men of his period than most whites can appreciate. His counterparts and he had to contend with far more confusing and tragic conditions than commonly thought, mostly due to limited public understanding of Indians in general and of the special kinds of problems they had to deal with.

What is certain is that Early, like his many of his contemporaries, was an extremely troubled man. Out in the Territory, this was not an uncommon problem.

FALLING INTO THE MIRE

FOR WHATEVER THE REASONS, Early Tiger was among the countless number of Indian men who fell into a dissolute way of life during the years after his tribe was removed to the Oklahoma Indian Territory. His affliction was to the extent that he ended up under the control of a wide range of harmful vices. For example, after his first use of tobacco, he smoked or chewed or dipped it from that point forward. Likewise, once he tried alcohol, it became a lifelong addiction. Most notable, after receiving his first handouts through programs sponsored by the federal Bureau of Indian Affairs, he refused to work hard for a living from then on. Long before he matured enough to give any rational thought to taking control of his own future, his pattern of life had been irretrievably set.

Most would blame Early's vices and subsequent shameful behavior solely on his own personal failings, but, as explained earlier, there were always some who did not see his situation as being that obvious or simple. According to these folks, heaping all the blame for Indian problems on the backs of people like Early was nothing but a knee-jerk reaction. They believed that at least some part of the difficulties they got into was rooted in the circumstances of their overall environment. "It isn't far-fetched," they argued, "that at least some small part of the misfortune men like Early had to deal with stemmed from realities associated with growing up during a period when Indians were left with little choice but to live a second-class existence, having to abide by the rules and values of people they hated having to deal with and didn't respect."

At the risk of idealizing or romanticizing Early's many faults and failures, it does seem unreasonable to think that he might have been one of those Indians who did not respond well to being physically as well as emotionally bowled over by superior authority and power. This may be part of the explanation for his having capitulated to the sense of hopelessness that had stalked him for years. In other words, he may have reacted and behaved much like many of the peers and elders that made up his reference groups. It does not seem unreasonable to think that a subliminal reaction of this kind might have had at least some impact on his becoming the way he was.

In the end, though, what is indisputable is that his life eventually dissolved into a haze of alcohol-induced slovenliness and indolence, regardless of how or why his problems evolved into existence. Folks in and around town eventually came to think of him as a local wastrel, a completely dissolute character. He became a well-known figure, especially to local authorities and informal community leaders who had to deal with the effects of his antisocial behavior. He was in one kind of trouble or another almost all the time, repeating the same dumb mistakes and misdemeanors as if he were on a treadmill.

Whenever he went on a spree and once again turned himself into a public nuisance, authorities would haul him off to jail and leave him there long enough to sleep it off. As soon as he recovered enough to be released, they knew all too well that in short order he would get drunk again and the whole process would be repeated. It became an endless cycle, but with each iteration his behavior became a little more disturbing and his crimes became a little more serious.

Over the years, Early evolved into a notorious local pest, a man well known for spending much of his time immersed in a haze of drunkenness and dissolution. Local authorities, Indians as well as white, considered him to be a hopelessly aimless, drunken sot. Responsible citizens, Indian and white alike, people who had their own lives under control, considered him to be a man without character. It is easy to confirm that he was viewed in this way, since he attested to it himself, in the article that was written about his life.

During the years when Early's problems were still evolving, residents as well as the official and unofficial authority figures of the area did no more than downplay his antics and ridicule them behind his back. Later, when he started doing things that could no longer be described as humorous, all their laughing stopped.

It came as no surprise to anyone when they heard during the investigation that Mock's peers saw her dealings with him as being, in their own words, "So stupid that she had to be as crazy as he was." It was wise of the girls to view interaction with Early in that light, since it truly would have been risky business for any young woman of their age and experience to get involved with a guy like him.

It is too late now to do any more than speculate about what forces may or may not have driven Early's destructively antisocial behavior, but even today, there would most likely be some mental health specialists who might maintain that the circumstances his people were caught up in were at least partially responsible for his having, as they would put it, acted out, the way he did. It certainly does not require much of a stretch to buy into the thought that he might have been embittered against of the powers that circumscribed his daily life — white or tribal authorities alike. At the risk of coming across as an apologist for his appalling behavior, it does seem reasonable to think that he had to live under conditions that would have been hard for lots of men to swallow.

A FAR
FROM NOBLE INDIAN

THE OVERRIDING REALITY that was crystal clear to one and all by this point in Early's life was that his temperament and personality had changed over the years in ways that belied the romanticized image of the noble Indian as it is commonly depicted. Even a brief review of the record that exists for him is enough to see that he was neither noble nor brave, not even in the broadest senses of the terms. On the contrary, with the passage of time he evolved into a dangerous person, a man who, as folks would have said back then, had to be watched out for and to never turn your back on. It was well known that he was wound up way too tightly, and that he had turned into a man who could never be fully trusted. Even his drinking and gambling buddies, his casual peers, viewed him in this way.

Over the years, Early's reputation grew in notoriety for another reason as well, a reason in addition to his well-known proclivities for drinking and gambling and the like. It grew out of the kind of freelance work he did to earn goods in trade and, on occasion, a little cash income. Through this work, he came to be viewed as an unusually cruel human being. That people began to think of him in this way added a whole new negative dimension to his already rotten reputation.

The kind of work he did was not what worsened his reputation; it was the way he did it. He was a horse trainer, which, of course, was in no way unusual in his setting, but he employed training techniques that were exactly that: unusual. He techniques anything but common place, as far as most of his neighbors were concerned. Those who knew only a little about his practices had no reservations about them, but they were repulsive to those who did.

His methods were labor intensive and required a great deal of attentive persistence, but they were effective without fail. When an unbroken horse landed in his care through trade or for hire, training began with securing it to a solid post using a rope halter that was thrown over its head and muzzle. Once he had a sure grip on the rope, he would gradually draw it closer and closer to him, all the while maintaining the post as a safety barrier between him and the horse. Very visible on the ground beside the security post, he kept what he referred to as a training stick, a tapered switch about a yard long and around three-quarters of an inch thick at its base. Wherever they were, animals were always in line of sight of it; Early made sure of that.

Steadily and carefully, he would pull the untrained horse closer and closer to the post that stood between them, watching it become increasingly panic-stricken as the space between them narrowed. When the horse was up close to the post and tightly secured by means of a now short tether, he would whip it about the mouth, face, neck, and flanks. The more the animal was struck, the more terrified it would become. It would fight and struggle with all its might to get away, but, of course, escape was an impossibility.

The switching would continue for as long as it took for either the horse or he to require a moment of rest. It stopped only when the horse stood still for a moment, quivering in fear of the stick. If the animal continued to resist, he would resume the whipping and wait for another pause. Sooner or later, it wound up battered and bruised into exhausted submission. Eventually, even the slowest of horses figured out that only by standing still, panting, shuddering, and staring in abject terror, could they avoid continued application of the training stick that Early always held upright and kept visible in his hand. After the animal was reduced in this way, it was set free and allowed to stumble out to pasture. As it was being fed the next morning, it would be reharnessed and training would start all over again, in every way as brutally as before.

Early knew that every horse would eventually begin to react the same way: They would cower and freeze in abject fear at the very sight of the upraised stick, so terrified that their eyes would follow any movement he made with it. They tended to stay that way, too, until the stick was out of their line of sight.

Through continued training of this kind, even the dumbest of dumb animals, from Early's perspective, would eventually figure out that making any twitch without his approval would lead to yet another beating. With enough exposure to this brutal but highly effective regimen, horses he was hired to train learned that it was wise to move only as commanded. Horses for drayage as well as those used for saddling and riding were broken using this and other effective but equally appalling and brutal techniques.

Early's view was that his efforts produced thoroughly trained animals, horses that could be used for riding or harnessed for drayage or sold for a profit. As far as he was concerned, he was providing a valuable service. The fact that the animals brought to him were more broken down than trained was a fine point that was of little or no concern to him, any more than it was to some of his customers. Any criticisms that were leveled against his methods were, to his way of thinking, frivolous as well as silly. He was unapologetically proud of the quality of his work, although he knew that some residents of the community considered his techniques to be exceptionally callous and cruel.

Eventually, every horse that came to him was trained up to his standards of satisfaction, even if that meant that some of them wound up with cracks in an occipital orb or an ear hanging limply at the side of the head. Early had no qualms about beating an animal bloody, especially those that angered him to the point of his losing patience with them. This happened often, mainly because he had extraordinarily little patience to begin with. His perspective on training was that there would always be more horses, so what did it matter how the few that were not amenable to his methods and, therefore, to his way of thinking, of lower value, were treated. To him they were nothing but dumb animals, and he really didn't care if an animal was brutalized or not.

Early's problem was that although some members of the community were indifferent to or even impressed by his training techniques, even more were totally put off by the way he treated animals. It became yet another example of behavior on his part that did not garner respect. It became one more entry on a long list of reasons why many local people, behind his back, had begun referring to him as "Crazy Early."

When Early finally got word of this new moniker, it became yet another justification for the bitterness that was growing within him. It was well known that he resented any criticism of his training techniques, in the same way that he resented criticism of himself as a person. In his view, any comment made against him was affront that deserved to be dealt with, and he was always ready to argue or fight. Whenever he thought someone was putting him down, he would become even more edgy and explosive than normal. This was especially true when he was drunk, and he had gradually gotten to a point of staying drunk whenever he could afford to buy alcohol.

When Early discovered that no other path was open to him, he decided that he had no choice but to get used to living life as a loner. Only boozers like himself were willing to hang around with a person as besotted and volatile as he was. Whether he liked it or not, he had become an odd man out around town, a person that others stayed away from whenever they could.

Early was aware of how people felt about him, but he never could muster enough willpower to do what was required to make his life any better. The only members of the community who were willing to buddy up with him were other sloppy drunks, guys who had the same kind of problems he did. When it became obvious to him that folks in town had begun to avoid him like the plague, that behavior became yet another excuse for his growing anger toward those who lived around and about him. He resented how he was treated, and he was more than willing to let people know it. From his perspective, belligerence toward others was nothing more than another way of standing up for himself.

When he figured out how people were treating him, he did not take it very well. In fact, he saw it as one more justification for hating his two-faced neighbors, as another unfair aggravation to embitter him even more. Okay, he thought to himself, let them do what they will. If others choose to avoid or ignore me, then so be it. In his mind, unofficial shunning became additional justification for his already far out of hand tendencies to drink to excess whenever he could, to steal whatever he could get his hands on, and to cause as much trouble as he could get away with. Neither Early nor anyone else in the community kept track of how his many problems came about, but with the passage of time it became ever more obvious that he had become more bitter and venomous than ever.

His problems were also complicated by his being

totally uneducated and untrained, and like many Indians in his surroundings, highly superstitious. For example, when he felt angry or threatened while he was drunk, he was known to blame unseen and unknown forces — spirits that were determined to make his life as miserable as they could. One constant of his life was that he never blamed himself for anything. With each new misery that befell him, be became more willing to lash out violently whenever he thought he could get away with it.

Exaggerated by ever-growing alcoholism, his condition continued to worsen as his life drifted by. Softer-hearted members of the community still conjectured about how being overcome by subconscious anger was at the root of his many fears, doubts, and shortcomings, but even these folks, along with those who did not hold their point of view, eventually became more wary and afraid of him with every day that passed. In short, Early gradually evolved from being a harmless town drunk into someone who could, confronted by the right set of circumstances, become a real danger to any one in town. He had become, as some would have put it back then, a living and breathing instance of the proverbial accident about ready to happen.

Despite his awful person habits and generally horrible reputation, Early took up with a series of Creek Indian women over the years. He had long-termed relationships with two of them as common law wives, and, some thought, fathered at least two children, although he refused paternity and claimed neither of the kids as his own. His "wives" eventually walked out on him, in both cases after claiming they had been beaten and abused. The two of them had moved away with their children, intent on making new lives someplace else. They never looked back, since their thoughts about him after their respective departures had been reducible to two short words: Good riddance!

After each of his separations, Early's drunkenness and outbursts of anger became more frightening than ever before, to the extent of others being able to see that he was becoming more and more emotionally unhinged. Inner emotional stress combined with alcohol poisoning can have that kind of effect on a human being. In his own way, he did try to restrain himself, not as a matter of principle but solely for the purpose of staying out of trouble. His problem, though, was that he was never was able to avoid his principal vice, drunkenness, and therefore never got his temper under control. He got involved in incident after incident that led to run-ins with the law, with each one becoming a little more serious than the one before.

Residents of the community continually asked: "What ought to be done about him?" Folks no longer doubted that, under the right set of circumstances, he could be a danger to any one of them. In the end, though, the practical matter of deciding how he ought to be dealt with was never openly confronted. That was unfortunate, since events were about to prove that those who had been worried about how he might fly of the handle and do some terrible thing could not have been any more correct.

MICKEY J. "MIKE" MARTIN

A MISTAKENLY
FORMED IMPRESSION

MAY 13 OF 1882 was the evening of the fateful stomp. When Mock and Early climbed aboard Harley Wilson's freight wagon to take advantage of his low-cost ride over to the stomp grounds out past Hitchita, they were not fit for participation in a social occasion of any kind, much less one at which the probability of a lot of drinking and wild partying taking place was nearly 100 percent. Unlike their fellow revelers, their moods were so sour that they were likely to have trouble getting along with anyone.

A number of those who showed up at the barn for the ride over to the event were near carbon copies of Early, in that they were nearly fully drunk even before they piled aboard the wagon. Others began drinking soon after they got seated, in most cases even before the rig pulled away from the stable. Their revelry began with bottles of home-brewed beer and mason jars of homemade whiskey that were passed around at will. To no one's surprise, the drinking continued with unanimous approval throughout the ride over.

By the time the wagon arrived at the fairgrounds, most of the revelers had had a lot to drink and many were happily as high as kites. Mock, like the others, had accepted a few drinks on the way over, but she had been more conservative about it than most. She had expected to see plenty of drinking, but the amount of it that had taken place within the confines of the wagon bed before they even reached their destination caught her completely off guard.

Mock and Early sat diagonally across from one another in the bed of the wagon during the ride over. He swallowed whiskey from his own jug all the while. Staring fixedly at her throughout the trip, he tried his best to lock eyes with her, command her attention, and launch a conversation. She, on the other hand, had studiously avoided looking in his direction and tried her absolute best to avoid any level of overt interaction, nothing past a brief initial brief hello.

Mock knew right away that her reaction to Early's overtures had irritated him, but instinct told her that that was the way it had to be. She knew it would be a mistake to offer the least amount of encouragement, considering the state he was in, and that was the last thing she wanted to do. In the bed of the wagon during their trip to the dance, the two of them had been, as far as she was concerned, way too close for comfort.

It did not occur to Early that because he was much older than Mock, she would not want to encouragement him in any way. Instead, he found it as aggravating as hell that not a single word had passed between them during the ride to the dance — nothing, once again, after their casual initial greeting.

She had bantered and always been very friendly toward him around town in the past, and that made

Early wonder why there wasn't more of that kind of thing now, when they were about to be right in the big middle of a social setting. The more he thought about her behavior, the more irritated he became. What damned reason, he thought to himself, does she have to dismiss me that way? Very clearly, he viewed the relationship between them, as tentative as may have been, in one way, while she looked at it in quite another.

Unbeknownst to Mock, Early also paid a great deal of attention to Mock's unspoken demeanor, not only during the ride over but also later during evening as well. One thing he noted was how agitated she seemed to be, and he couldn't help but wonder why. On top of that, he noticed that she spent most of the evening on the sidelines, wistfully looking on while others danced, laughed, and hooted the night away. His impression was that she wanted to be a lot more involved in the action than she was bold enough to be. She most definitely wants a lot more that she's getting, he thought to himself.

On May 13, 1882, Early was forty-two to Mock's twenty years of age. They'd been brought together that night because, truth be known, there was so precious little to do for fun in their remote area of the Nation. Those who were in the market for entertainment had no choice but to take part in whatever happened to be going on at a given moment, no matter what age bracket they happened to be in. That evening, the dance at the stomp grounds out past Hitchita was where the action was, so that was where people of all ages ended up going.

Mock and Early's rural community was nothing more than a sleepy little village, one of a string of others just like it elsewhere in their remote region of the Territory. It was located, like the Creek capital city itself, within the section of the country that in later years would become known as the Bible Belt. It was right near the geographical center of the Creek Nation, about 75 miles south of the larger town of Tulsa.

Residents of small communities like theirs were accustomed to traveling by horseback or wagon to towns such as Henryetta or Okmulgee, their national capital, for all sorts of purposes. That is why the ride over to the stomp site in Harley Wilson's freight wagon was considered an acceptable haul.

Neither Early nor Mock was well thought of within their settlement, but it must be noted at this juncture that their negative reputations were formed in ways that were as different as night and day. Her bad reputation had grown up out of the clay of extreme youthful immaturity, while his, described as bluntly as is deserved, was formed out of real dirt.

There is a huge difference, as we all know, between the kind of "badness" that grows out of the petulant obnoxiousness of youth and the kind that oozes forth due to truly longstanding and deep-seated personal problems. Those members of the community who had paid even a modest level of attention to Early's behavior over the years knew that he suffered from proclivities and afflictions that all too definitely belonged in the latter category. His problem, as anyone in the community readily would have pointed out, was that he had had to deal with emotional issues that were way too complicated for him or, for that matter, anyone else in town to comprehend. No one could even describe his overall problem, much less explain it, at least not with any degree of clarity.

That Mock and Early were well known to be troubled individuals was an observation that civic authorities would not have hesitated to make, had anyone happened to ask them. In addition, most anyone who knew them would have added that while her behavior might have righted itself if she had had a chance to grow a little older, his condition was well past any reasonability possibility of repair. He was too far gone, most people would have said, for there to be any realistic chance of straightening him out.

Once Early finally realized that people had begun to avoid him whenever they could, he had grown angrier than ever. Whenever he engaged in discussion with anyone, his eyes mirrored exactly what he was thinking, which, typically, was: Who in the hell does this character think he or she is. Always on the edge of outright hostility, he never as much as considered asking himself why so many of his neighbors dealt with him the way they did. He wasn't focused enough to engage in the kind of introspective questioning that might have been of some help to him. That kind of thing was not part of his makeup.

About the only thing Early was good at was hating other people, and he did an awful lot of that. Bitterness and anger had grown worse within him day by day, until, by the date of the stomp, he was a powder keg about ready to explode. It had become obvious to one and all that he was a dangerous guy to be around.

Many people knew that he had trouble controlling himself, but not a one of them knew what to do about it. A man cannot be punished for what he might do, as we all know. Other than waiting to see if punishable offenses were committed, what could have been done? Not a single resident of the community had even close to the level of insight that would have been required to understand, much less actually help, such a benighted man. What this meant, in the end, was that nothing was done about him. People figured that the law would take over if he got too far out of hand. At that point, his condition would either be turned around or he would be thrown back in jail, hopefully for a very long time.

It was a point of near unanimous concurrence within the community that he might go off at any moment, for any one of a whole host of possible reasons. It was also agreed that he had long since become his own worst enemy. No one even remotely understood how things had disintegrated to such a low point; the answer to that question was complete mystery. Even after taking this into account, there was no mechanism in place for anyone in town to even as much as think of questioning Early's right, as dangerous as he was, to get stone cold drunk and take part in the stomp out past Hitchita.

AN UNFORTUNATE CROSSING OF PATHS

THINGS CAME TO A HEAD for Early "Hawk" Tiger and Etta "Mock" Burnham during the early morning hours of the night of the stomp. They, along with others, began making their separate ways back toward where the wagon team was tethered for the trip back to Wilson's barn and from there on to their personal homes. The stomp was still going on, but the hour for their departure had been prearranged. Now that their involvement revelry was over, the travelers were tired. All they wanted was to get home and hit the sack.

Mock was in good spirits and somewhat giddy due to having imbibed more than she knew she should have, but she was still well in control of herself. She was not stone cold drunk, in other words, like many of her fellow travelers as they headed for the rally point. Early, though, was so inebriated that he stumbled as he walked, cursing under his breath all the while. It was not unusual for him to behave that way, since he got drunk whenever he had a dollar to spend.

Mock would have had no way of knowing that on top of how drunk he was, Early was boiling with anger over the way things had gone for him during the evening. Every woman he tried to buddy up with had put him off, which turned the whole damned stomp into another evening of the same kind of rejection he had had to put up for most of his recent life. If there is anything I hate, he thought to himself as he bumbled along the path toward the wagon, it's stuck-up women! Seething with resentment, he wished he could think of some good ways of evening the score.

Mock and Early's paths crossed — or, more likely, seemed to have crossed — as they walked toward where Wilson's team was tethered and waiting. He didn't waste a moment before trying to take advantage of their seemingly chance meeting by attempting to strike up what he envisioned as being a little friendly conversation. Casually throwing an arm over her shoulder, he tried to talk with her about what she thought of the dance.

Put off by the drunken advance she knew he was trying to pass off as spirited friendliness, Mock said in the boldest and most forceful voice she could sum up: "Get your dirty hands off me, you disgusting drunk!" and then, after letting him know exactly how she felt about what he was doing, she forcefully threw his arm off her shoulder, shoved him away as best she could, and attempted to spin out of his grasp.

Tragically for her, things did not go as well for her as they usually did when she put her foot down and spoke out loudly and forcefully. People such as her parents or acquaintances of her own age usually backed off after that. In this situation, much to her surprise, open anger and loud protestations did not have the effect she expected. Instead, it had absolutely no discernable impact, not in terms of cowing a person as soused and as angry as Early was in the heat of the moment.

Neither her words nor her response went over well with him, since they so very plainly demonstrated that she was put off by him altogether. Her behavior came across as another betrayal. As far as he was concerned, he had done nothing wrong — nothing that warranted the kind of cold-shouldering he was getting from Mock. Sick and tired of being rejected at every turn, he had taken all he could, not only from Mock but from others across the board. Angry and drunk well beyond any normal level of inhibition, his reaction was as immediate as it was thoughtless.

Incensed by how he had been rebuffed, he grabbed Mock by one arm and drug her kicking and screaming out into one of the small groves of saplings that lined the pathway back to the wagon. As soon as he got her out of sight of the trail, he slung her to the ground and, after she was down, went down on his own knees and began to grope and fondle her. Then, as drunk as he was, he started pulling up her blouse.

Further angered when she continued to resist and scream, he repeatedly backhanded her across the face and told her to shut the hell up. When she still refused to get into what he thought to be the appropriated spirit of the moment, his open-handed slapping quickly turned into closed fist punches, which continued until Mock became so frozen in fear that she stopped fighting altogether. She had initially reacted in anger, but it was not long before her rage was replaced by outright terror.

Crazy Early was a scary guy even when he was not angry or drunk, and by this point it had become clear to Mock that he was not only angry and drunk but absolutely enraged as well. She realized that he did not understand how much he had hurt her, nor did he comprehend how close he was hurting even more severely. What flashed through her mind was that he was acting exactly like the kind of crazy man others had said he was. Trembling in fear, she stopped resisting and became as limp as a rag.

As soon as he saw that she was helpless and compliant, he pulled her skirt up over her face, ripped off her undergarments, and raped her. It was over in only a matter of minutes. It happened so quickly that Mock was unable to fully comprehend what was happening to her. Having been beaten half senseless, lucid thought had become impossible.

When he was through with her, he stood up, unsteadily buttoned his pants, snarled a warning for her to keep her damned mouth shut about what "they" had done, and then stumbled off toward the path that led back to where the wagon and team were waiting for the trip home. He left her there alone, lying in a heap, rolling in grass, leaves, and dirt, gasping in fright, and crying her eyes out, her clothing pulled up toward a bruised and bloody face.

Mock was as shocked by the gravity of the crime

that had been committed against her as he was oblivious to it. To put it bluntly, her violation had been so unexpected and so great that she was unable to absorb the truth of it and react in any way close to the manner that was warranted. It had happened so much out of the blue and in such a matter-of-fact way that she was left bewildered. In a sense, it was hard to accept that it had even happened. She knew without doubt that it had not mattered much to her attacker; his behavior had clearly demonstrated that.

More confused and forlorn than openly angry, Mock struggled to take in what had happened. That the act had been committed by a person over twice her age, a man she knew of and had joked with in the past but that she could not say that she really knew — at least not beyond the level of friendly bantering — made it even more impossible to believe. That such a thing had happened to her, of all people, did not mesh with the way she conceptualized herself, since it so obviously clashed with the always-ready-to-fight reputation she had so diligently worked on and built up over the years. I'm supposed to be a tough one, she thought, so how in the world could such a thing have happened to me, of all people? With these fleeting thoughts coursing through her mind and feeling as if she had fallen off a horse, Mock eventually realized that she had no alternative but to stop crying and get back up on her feet. After wandering around in aimless hand-wringing circles for a little while, she rearranged her clothing, cleaned off her face with spittle, and straightened her hair as best she could. When those steps were completed, she walked shakily out of the grove of saplings and headed off down the same path Early had taken a few short minutes before. She did not know what else to do. It was late, she was shaken and ragged, and there was no other place for her to go but home.

Upon arrival at the wagon for the ride back over to Wilson's barn, she saw that he was already on board. The ride home took place in as uncomfortable proximity as the ride over, swaying along on the wagon in the company of others whose revelry during the evening had been way too hearty. Her fellow passengers were either too drunk or too tired to talk to or pay much attention to anyone but themselves. Now that the stomp was over, all they wanted to do was get home and fall into bed. Early was passed out cold throughout the trip, lying flat out in the bed of the wagon. Tipsy and stunned, Mock stared directly at her rapist all the way back to the barn, still too much in shock to express any outward anger.

More than anything else, Mock was overwhelmed and confused by what had happened. She could not bring herself to utter a peep to anyone about what Early had done. Nobody on the wagon with them that night had any idea they had ridden home literally rubbing shoulders with a rapist and his victim. If Mock had wanted to cry out about what happened, she should have done it right away, certainly before the evening was over. As obvious as this would have been to any dispassionate observer, she did not say a word about it to anyone.

MOCK DEALS WITH
HER SITUATION

ORDINARILY, AN ACT of unprovoked violence such as the rape of a young woman would have outraged the residents of a community in which it took place, but nothing of the kind occurred after what happened to Mock. In truth, there was no reaction to the incident at all, simply because she decided of her own accord not to mention it to a single soul, especially not to members of her own family. They, in fact, as far as Mock was concerned, were the very ones she most wanted not to know anything about what had happened.

She knew all too well that she had a reputation for flirtatious behavior as well as outright promiscuity around town. She deserved it, too, she had to admit. In the past, knowing that this was so had been nothing more than something else she chose to laugh about, knowing that one day she was going to leave her hometown and never come back. What did it matter, therefore, whether local people — or, for that matter, members of her own family — had high regard for her or not? Now, though, in view of what had happened, her lack of a good reputation did not seem so funny. This was the very type of behavior, she recalled, her folks had warned her against, no more than a few minutes before her departure for the stomp. She cringed at the thought of what they were sure to say, if they were to learn what had happened.

Her response to them back then, she dejectedly and painfully remembered, had been to laugh in their faces and tell where to get off. She had told them, in fact, that they ought to mind their own damned business. Why in the world, she asked herself, was I so insolent and arrogant? She knew even then that her folks were only trying to look out for her.

Now that the chickens had come home to roost, Mock was too embarrassed and confused to seriously consider telling her parents that she had been raped. Instead, she came up with a scheme to conceal the truth about what had happened, a concocted story she thought would be clever enough to fool anyone who heard it. It would be that a drunk had tried to force himself on her, which was certainly true, but only as far as it went. The remainder of her story was an out and out lie.

"I fought like hell when he tried to grab me," she declared when she finally talked with them, and then further embellishing her account of what had happened by bragging about having won the struggle against her drunken attacker. "You should have seen the guy when it was over," she laughed; "I may look bad, but he probably looked a whole lot worse. I didn't get a good look at how badly he was hurt, since it was dark, and we were both drunk. The one thing that's for certain is that he sure as hell didn't bother me after that!"

Her artlessly calculated remarks were designed to

fend off any detailed questioning by family members and acquaintance alike as well as to impress others by describing how resolute and tough she had been. She said what she felt compelled to say, but her entire account of what had happened was nothing more than a pack of lies.

Maintaining a don't mess with me persona was of such paramount importance to Mock that she had spent years cultivating a reputation for toughness among her peers. The last thing she wanted to do was give all that up. For Mock, having been physically assaulted dramatically clashed with her concept of self. She could not face the thought of admitting to the reality of what had taken place.

It was as clear as a bell to those who listened to her story that she had been involved in a down and dirty altercation of one kind or another, since there was evidence aplenty of exactly that: her eyes were blackened, her lips were fat and swollen, scratches were visible on her hands and arms and neck, her clothes were ripped, and she complained of being stiff all over. She had been in a fight; there was no doubt about that. Most listeners believed what she had to say, but only up to a point.

From Mock's first description of the incident and from that point forward, people were skeptical about large portions of what she said. Members of her own family, for example, most specifically her own father and mother, were among her greatest doubters. Because she had lied to them so often in the past, they took for granted that she was more than willing to lie to them again. What stumped them was that they could not figure out how or why.

In the end, her parents, relatives, and acquaintances concluded that it was okay not to probe the matter any further. Although Mock clearly had gotten into in a fight and been beaten up, no permanent harm had been done and maybe, hopefully, they thought to themselves, she might have learned a lesson that would turn her around for the better. With this hopeful thought in mind, her significant others, much to Mock's relief, let the matter drop and said nothing further about it.

MOCK'S
EYES FINALLY OPEN

IN WHAT SEEMED like no more than a few days but was really several months, Mock, to her great surprise and utter dismay, figured out due to unmistakable signs that she had become pregnant. It had to have been a result of Early's attack that night at the stomp, she realized, since there had been no one else.

She found it almost impossible to believe that so momentous a consequence could have resulted from an event as sordid and meaningless as their coming together, but there it was, whether she wanted it to be so or not. Moreover, it had also become clear that she would not be able to conceal her condition much longer.

Totally mortified by fearful thoughts of what she knew her parents' reaction was going to be, Mock was overcome with despair. She was so upset she could not eat or sleep, much less come up with any clear thoughts about how to deal with her predicament. She painfully recalled that her parents and others had told her at least a million times that this was what could happen, and now here she was, caught up right in the big middle of exactly what they had warned her against. Me, she thought to herself yet again, of all people!

It was a mess of her own making, she realized, knowing that if she had listened to her parents, she would not have been at the stomp in the first place. It was clear that her folks had been right all along, although it was too late for the admission to be of any help to her at that point.

Knowing that she ought to have thought things over and been much more careful, she couldn't stop berating herself. It was her fault and nobody else's, and she should have come to her senses much earlier. How often had she been warned against engaging in any kind of interaction with Crazy Early? Too many to count, she had to admit. Further, how often had she been cautioned that smart mouthing the wrong person might get her into all sorts of trouble? Again, many. And how often had she been told how ill-advised it was for her go alone to a stomp at a site where things were known to get out of control on a regular basis? Too many to count, she remembered, just by her parents alone, not to mention others.

After going on and on in this vein for days on end, it finally dawned on Mock that disrespect and willful disobedience on her own part had been the primary cause of the mess she was in. Her parents had had her best interests at heart all along. Having to admit to them what condition she was in, she realized, was unavoidable, since, when you got right down to it, they were the only ones she had to turn to.

What she had to do was clear, but just thinking about how her folks were going to react left her feeling shaky and wobbly in the knees. As dreadful as confessing to them was going to be, she saw that no choice was open to her but to admit to her condition and face the inevitable consequences.

A PAINFUL CONFESSION

MOCK WAS DEAD RIGHT about what would happen. Her worst fears were realized when she explained her condition to her folks. They reacted just angrily as she thought they would; in fact, they had a full-fledged conniption fit.

They were unsurprised to hear that she had been lying when she said she had been involved in a fight at the stomp, since they had suspected as much as the tale was spun. What they could not understand, however, was why in the world she had not spoken out immediately after the assault? Why would she not have cried out to high heaven, they wondered, when that is exactly what anyone else in her position would have done. Because she had not done so, their immediate reaction was that a whole lot more had taken place that night than what she'd told them. They were convinced that, even now, she still was not telling them the full truth. They knew very well that she had lied to them many times in the past, even about situations not nearly as mind-boggling and portentous as this one.

When Mock tried to explain how she got into her condition by casting all blame for it on local miscreant Early Tiger, her parents did not believe she was telling them the full truth. They were convinced that that such an incident could not have taken place as Mock claimed. If she had been a totally innocent victim, they reasoned, she would have gone to the authorities or to them immediately after the attack. It was inconceivable to them that a person as outspoken and audacious as their daughter would not have come forward as quickly as possible. "Any fool," they blared, "would have had enough sense to do something as obvious as that."

What was immediately obvious to them was that all Mock would be able to do at that late date if Early were accused of rape would be to offer up her word against his and that anything she might say would be viewed as suspect by anyone who heard it. It was too late in the game, they realized, to prove that Crazy Early had committed an offense against her at all. The man truly would have to be crazy, they understood, not to react to any accusation she might level against him by denying it altogether.

Anyone could have gotten her pregnant, they could almost hear the man saying, which would lead to even more humiliation being heaped upon their family than if the responsibility for her condition was clearly determinable. Their neighbors, they feared, would most likely believe him if he reacted in that way, since the whole town was aware of how Mock had behaved in the past. It would not be the first accusation of promiscuity that had been leveled against their daughter, and they knew how agonizing it would be to have to admit that it was true.

Beyond the fact of Early Tiger being an odd guy

with a notably unsavory reputation, and that some people in the community addressed him as "Hawk," although other referred to him in private as "Crazy Early," Andy and Ruby didn't know a single thing about the man. All they knew with certainty was that their daughter had a well-deserved reputation for wayward behavior, and that when a situation as salacious as this one became general knowledge, residents of their town would gossip about them forever. For them, that was an awful thought, one that settled over their lives like a dark cloud that had the weight of a ton of bricks.

Their overall reaction to Mock's accusation against Early was stony disbelief that she had been the innocent victim of a totally unprovoked attack. She ought to have had enough common sense not to get involved with a man like him, not in any way, shape, or form. Bellowing without restraint, they demanded that she go to her "lover" and plead for him to accept her in marriage, since under no circumstances should a child be brought into the world out of wedlock.

"Every child," Andy thundered, "has to have a legal father." As far as Ruby and he were concerned, a backyard abortion was totally out of the question. "You made your damned bed," each of her parents reiterated loudly and forcefully, "and, by God, you have to get the hell back out there and sleep in it!"

Mock knew her parents' take on what had happened was completely off the mark, but she also realized that at that late date, so many months after the event, there was no way on earth she could prove it. She was unequivocally told that her only option was to, "Try to work things out with the man in your life."

Mock was so overwhelmed by feelings of desperation and anxiety that she panicked altogether. Although her folks were wrong about the particulars of the situation, she saw that there was no choice open to her but to think seriously about doing exactly what they had advised. Advice that at first seemed totally unreasonable, in other words, suddenly began to seem reasonable after all. She, like her parents, could see no other way out.

Like her folks, she knew it was true that in their tight-knit little community, girls who became pregnant out of wedlock were stigmatized and treated like lepers. They were considered fallen women, no more and no less, and that was how people would think of them forever. To Mock, it was a fate worse than death. Even marrying a man like Early Tiger, as far as she was concerned, would be preferable to living in the purgatory she would have to face as an unwed mother.

In isolated communities like hers, no social service agencies existed to help young women figure out how to deal with a predicament like hers. With her own family showing no sympathy and refusing to help in any way other than advising that she ought to deal with the situation by "working things out with her lover," Mock had little choice but to conclude they were telling her the gospel truth. She really did not have another option; the only way out was for her to subject herself to the tender mercies of the very man who had so mindlessly assaulted her, Early "Hawk" Tiger.

As bad as marriage to a twice-divorced character like Crazy Early might be, Mock reasoned, there was no other honorable way out of the mess she was in. Although she was afraid of the man and knew little more about him than who he was in the community, she decided that she had no alternative but to seek him out, explain her condition to him, and to insist upon his doing the right thing. He was going to be the father of her child, she reasoned, so he would have no choice but to marry her.

Having arrived at this decision ought to have made Mock feel a little better about things, but it didn't, not in the least. Due to an awful sense of foreboding, her spirit was not lifted in the slightest. Nearly overcome by feelings of desperation, she remained as depressed as she had ever been in her life. Her sense of gloom continued to grow, in the same way that it had for her family. She was already miserable, but now she hit rock bottom. She finally saw that what her parent had suggested would have to be done, but she dreaded with all her heart having to do it.

SLAPPED IN THE FACE
BY REALITY

AFTER SUMMONING UP every scrap of courage she could muster, a miserably dejected and thoroughly unnerved but determinedly dutiful Mock trudged away from her family home. She set out on miles of unpaved road, walking the dusty miles through her rural community that had to be traversed to reach the isolated piece of property that belonged to Early Tiger, the man who had so greatly wronged her only a few short months before. She knew exactly where he lived, as did everyone else in the area. She knew, too, that he lived alone, in a run-down old shack of a place that was even more scraggly looking than the unkempt land on which it stood.

After a few hours or so, she arrived at the front door of Early's home. She paused for a few minutes on his stoop, her chin down on her chest, her heart beating a mile a minute, and her mind spinning in trepidation. After pulling herself together as best she could, she began to knock, timidly at first but then more forcefully.

Just as soon as Early opened his door and stood before her in his entry way, Mock launched into a tearful and emotional explanation of what she had deluded herself into believing he would think of as their tragic situation. Bawling openly as she spoke, she told him about her condition. Then, in terms as forceful as she could summon up, and in the tone her parents had instructed her to use, she demanded that he accept the responsibility of patrimony and take on his rightful role as the father of their child. Beginning hesitantly, but then with greater stridency as the story flowed out of her, she pleaded with him not to leave her to deal with their situation alone.

Early was as knocked back on his heels upon learning of her condition as Mock had been herself, back when she first became aware of it, only a few months earlier. In shock over what she said, he stood before her in open-mouthed amazement, wondering if what she was saying might really be true. How in the world could it be, though? he thought to himself. He had been with the damned girl for only a few minutes on one miserable evening, minutes that he could hardly even remember. The one thing he did remember very well was how blasted angry he had been when she cold-shouldered him as if he were a total stranger. Who the hell did she think she was? he asked himself.

Early had to tax his mind before he could recall much more about what had taken place that night at the dance, but, after he did begin to remember, the central thought that jumped into his mind was how she had been only one of a series of stuck-up women who snubbed him that evening. Thinking about how they treated him outraged him all over again. The last very thing I ought to do, he thought to himself, is start feeling sorry for any one of those sorry bitches.

Why in holy hell, he thought after collecting him-self for a while, do things like this always happen to me? How did his drinking buddies Jack and Dub and Demp-sey always manage to dodge bullets of this kind, when I never can? Why, he silently lamented, do things like this always have to happen to me? Hearing that a baby was about to be born, a baby that well might be his own, did not resonate with him in any way that was helpful. That, he had decided in no more than an instant, was going to have to remain her problem, not his. Getting involved in her situation was the very last thing he in-tended to do.

Mock had seen in an instant that Early Tiger was never going to be anything close the kind of accommo-dating and understanding mature man she had prayed to encounter. He would never be anything like that, not even remotely so. It was as clear as a bell to her that accepting responsibility was not in the man's makeup, whether her accusation against him was true or not. Her condition, she realized, did not matter to him in the slightest, not even a whit.

Not only did he react poorly to Mock's entreaties, he also loudly and forcefully rejected any responsibility for her condition. He bluntly claimed that he hardly even knew who the hell she was, then said did not want to have a damned thing to do with her. "There's no way under the sun that I'm the father of your kid," he yelled, "and you have a hell of a lot of nerve making that kind of accusation against me!"

When Mock attempted to persist, he responded,

"You behave like a whore," he said. "Any man in town could be the father of your kid." Then, to make it crystal clear that bothering him any further would not do a speck of good, he slapped her face to make her to stop wailing. Then, he spun her around by the shoulders, kicked her in the butt, and told her to get the hell off his property. After that, he slammed his door shut behind her.

When Early slammed that door on her, Mock felt like her head was going to explode. She stood for a while on the walk that led away from his porch, nearly overcome by a gut-wrenching combination of embarrassment, grief, worry, and fear, all rolled up into one debilitating package. It was the worst day of her life, second only to the day of the rape itself. Her interaction with him could not have gone any worse than it had.

After standing a little longer on his walkway as if frozen in place, she turned around and slowly began the dusty trudge back to her parents and home, sobbing more with each step she took. Her situation seemed so hopeless that she felt like jumping off a bridge, for no reason other than to bring her misery to an end, once and for all.

It was not until this miserable juncture that Mock took full note of the reality of her situation. Her appeals for help had all been rejected, and she had appealed to every person she knew. Since she had enthusiastically burned as many bridges as she could think of, and then some, before getting into trouble, no one was willing to go to bat for her now when things started to go badly.

Not a single member of her family stepped forward to console or support her, and none of her fair-weather friends rose to her defense. No one had offered to help her in any way. For reasons she herself had invited, nobody wanted to get involved. She could not see even as much as a flicker of light to mitigate or stave off her all-enveloping gloom; all she saw before her was abject hopelessness.

THE ONLY
SENSIBLE SOLUTION

WITH HER DISHEVELED MIND now in even more of a scramble due to having been so humiliatingly rejected by Early, Mock's search for a way out of her dilemma grew more desperate with every hour that passed. Her I hope for a respectable solution had been nothing but a pipe dream. It was clear that Early was never going to be of any help to her, at least not without being forced to do so, and no one in town or even in the broader area had enough power to do that.

If the stark reality of her hopeless predicament had not been crystal clear before this point, it certainly was now. The stress of having to endure unending days of ever-increasing anxiety was close to becoming more than Mock could bear. Thinking clearly was impossible, and she was so tied up in knots that thoughts of bringing the whole miserable episode to an abrupt end began to sound more and more reasonable. Desperation, it is well known, can make a person think like that.

Thoughts zoomed through her head like birds in flight, most of them merely unrealistic but others nearly off the wall crazy. Thinking more like a trapped animal than a human being, a possibility she would not even have considered without having become desperate flitted into mind, a vision of how she might go about eliciting the kind of help she so urgently needed.

What had occurred to her was that she might ask for help from the only authority figures in the community who might be willing as well as able to intercede on her behalf, the missionary couple who for years had been active among the Indians of their locale. She could not envision what they might be able to do, but they seemed to be a good option, anyway. They were, as far as she knew at that moment, her only option.

She had said hello to them in passing, but she had had no other interaction with either of them. Her discussion of them with acquaintances in the past had been, well, mocking, in the same way that she tended to speak of almost everyone. There were very good reasons for people having begun calling her Mock.

The two people seemed decent enough, but all she knew about them other than how friendly they were was that they had well known reputations for doing good works in the vicinity. It was for this reason that they were so well respected. This being the case, she thought to herself, why not approach them? They were, truth be known, the only resource she had left to consider. All they could do if they did not want to help her, she reasoned, was say no. Considering what I'm up against, she thought to herself, what do I have to lose?

So, with no advance introduction or preamble of any kind, Mock made a beeline for the young couple's front doorstep. The second they opened their door to greet whoever was there to visit them, Mock launched into a tearful explanation of her forcible rape by Early a few months earlier, begging them for any assistance they might be able to provide. She was too overwhelmed with worry to care how she came across to anyone.

Mock saw no reason to hold anything back, since it had become apparent after only one short interaction with Early that if any accusation were leveled against him, he would not hesitate to rail right back against her, assassinating her character in any way he could. She knew and was fearful of what would happen if he was confronted but knew what she had to do so anyway. There was no way her problem was not going to become common knowledge, so there was nothing be gained by trying to be coy about the matter. Desperate problems call for desperate measures, she concluded, which meant that this was an occasion for doing exactly what had to be done, even if the very thought of it was repellant. A head-to-head confrontation with the man was unavoidable.

From that point forward, a record exists to show that Mock's impassioned appeal to the couple turned out to be highly effective. The two of them were proactive and industrious when it came to dealing with her predicament — at least, that is, for the short run. The short run, of course, was all Mock could think of at that juncture. What might happen after she was helped was the least of her worries, and it seems that consideration of longer termed consequences never crossed anyone else's mind, either. If they did, it had to have been only in the most cursory of ways.

If the approach the missionaries locked in on for dealing with Mock's situation had been considered from a long-term perspective, it might have occurred to someone that the solution they settled on might lead to an even greater mess for her later down the line. In the heat of the moment, though, the possibility of something of that kind happening in future years was the last thing on anyone's mind. In fact, no one gave it any serious thought, proving once again that there really are occasions when the road to hell is paved with good intentions.

From the outset of the couple's effort to help Mock, they were as suspicious as her own parents had been about why she had not reported her rape until months after the event — and, even then, not until she was so visibly pregnant that she had no choice. Like all of those she had spoken to, they were put off by all the lies she told, especially in terms of how she explained the incident to her parents, who clearly did not believe their own daughter. In short, the couple seemed to know a whole lot more about Mock's reputation within the community than they ever openly acknowledged.

From the standpoint of the two highly religious and obviously good-hearted missionaries, a baby's need for a father and a mother's need for a husband took precedence over taking sides with either Mock or Early. In their view, the needs of the child took precedence over all other considerations, no matter what might or might not take place in years to come.

Their conclusion, therefore, was that the worst

thing anyone could do at that juncture would be to take sides with either one of the principals. Each one of them, it was clear, had a different version of events to tell. Instead, they decided that all attention ought to be focused on moving toward the solution that seemed most reasonable under the circumstances. They settled on what they thought would work out best for the mother and child over the long haul, although they knew as well as anyone that it might very well lead to a less-than-stellar arrangement in later years.

They ignored or paid mere lip service to Early's highly vocal protestations of innocence. Instead, they proceeded to rally as much pressure as could be brought to bear into forcing him into doing what they were convinced ought to be done in the best interests of the mother, the unborn child, and the community. They made it very clear that they expected him to do the right thing by Mock, which was, in their minds, to marry her.

They were smart about it, too. By rallying forces behind the scenes, they pounded into his addled head how important it was for him to do what needed to be done and what they wanted him to do, although, legally speaking, no course of action was mandatory on his part or Mock's. Mock's parents, however, according to the record, were in full agreement with the resolution the missionary twosome put forth.

To put pressure on Early, the couple pulled together a group of local leaders to act as an unofficial quasi-judiciary review panel, whereupon Early and

Mock were called in for what was referred to as a "fact finding and discussion session." His participation was voluntary, he was told, but the whole idea of the effort was to create a setting in which pressure could be put on upon him. It worked, too, at least enough to get the job done. This was mainly because the panel was made up of the surly and grim-looking commanding officer of the detachment of U. S. Army troops on temporary duty in the area as well as several other leading members of the community. Once Early and Mock were standing before them, the group didn't waste a minute before getting down to brass tacks.

After a testy period of highly intensive probing, the domineering and highly influential missionaries and their equally influential associates extracted a confession from Early that he had had relations with Mock the evening of the stomp, several months back. He claimed, as would be expected, that their coming together had been consensual and he did not force her. He maintained that she had been even mor into than he was. "Ask her own friends," he said; "they'll verify how the two of us had been talking off and on for the better part of a year, despite the difference in our ages." Forcefully denying that he had committed an unwanted act against Mock, he claimed that she had been just as drunk and just as willing as he was, perhaps even more so.

After listening to both party's versions of events, those who were on hand for the session ended up more skeptical than ever about Early's protestations, especially after a few of Mock's relatives were brought in to describe in detail how bruised and beaten she had been the morning after the stomp. Nothing, they pointed out, would have been consensual about that.

EARLY GETS THE MESSAGE

IN THE END, what happened shortly thereafter is exactly what anyone familiar with the overall situation would have anticipated: Early buckled under the pressure of interrogation and censure when he finally got the message that formal charges could be brought against him if he refused to accept responsibility for having committed an offense against Mock. Perhaps because he feared yet another long stay in the grubby local jail or some other threat of retaliation against him, he finally saw the wisdom of helping Mock deal with her situation.

Although he protested, in 1882 Early was effectively shamed, cajoled, and threatened by local powers that be into marrying Mock. He also had to promise to provide for her, not for himself, but for the sake of the unborn child and its mother, whose needs, as far as the local leaders, especially the two missionaries, were concerned, trumped all other considerations.

Buckling under pressure, however, was a far cry from Early having been convinced that he ought to be held responsible for Mock's welfare, even if she was expecting. He never believed a word of it, not even for a minute.

Looking back at this sad affair many years after it happened, what seems apparent is that all members of the group of local leaders who helped deal with Mock and Early's situation had had nothing but disdain for the values and veracity of the two principals. To a person, each one of them seemed to have been disgusted by what had gone on before, during, and after the incident.

"If stripes was give out for bein' a damned reprobate," the blunt and outspoken army detachment leader who served on the panel was reported to have said, "that sonofabitch'd be a top sergeant!" Although none of the panelists ever said so openly, it seemed that all of them fully agreed with his sentiments.

Considering the values of their time and place and the stark realities inherent in the situation they had been called upon to deal with, the missionaries and other local authority figures who volunteered to help Mock deal with her situation deserved a good deal of credit. At the very least, they deserved praise for managing to calm the parties down enough for them to be able to talk with one another.

From the perspective of the local leaders, Mock needed a husband to provide a home for her unborn child while Early needed a good reason for getting control of the drunkenness and overall dissolute behavior that had turned him into a threat within their community. Obviously, convincing the two of them to marry was seen to be a clever backdoor means of solving two equally thorny local problems in a single stoke. Although they were antagonistic toward one another under present circumstances, their relationship, it was assumed, would improve as their marriage matured.

Local leaders settled on effectively forcing Early to marry Mock because that solution seemed to be the best way of providing for her and her unborn child over the long haul. Their take on the situation was that the welfare of the unborn child ought to provide enough incentive for the couple to come to their senses, grow up, and do what was right.

Most probably, not a one of those who urged Early and Mock to marry would have given any greater odds than a snowball's chance in hell of the two of them being able to make a success of it. The only reason no one said so while they were dealing with the issue was that not a one of them could think of a better option to place on the table.

THE FAMILY LIFE
OF TIGERS

NOT SURPRISINGLY, the marital relationship that evolved during the years that followed between Early Tiger and his hapless wife Mock ended up becoming what would have to be described as enduring one another when there was no way it could be avoided rather than as an actual marriage. It was a most pitiable union, one that overflowed with more private wretchedness than anyone would have imagined.

After Mock moved into Early's out-of-the-way, run-down place to begin their lives together, others hoped that as a legally married couple who would soon to have a child to care for that they would settle down and begin to work out answers for whatever problems might come up. That, though, is far from what really happened. Yes, they were man and wife in a legal sense, but it turned out to be nothing more than wishful thinking to assume they would look out for one another.

They had all kinds of problems, beginning with the handicap of no one in the community, after Early and Mock were defined, so to speak, as an established couple, wanting to have another thing to do with either one of them. As far as their neighbors were concerned, the two of them needed to learn to make it on their own. Even before they were pushed into marriage, their past bad behavior had alienated almost everyone they knew.

The communal take on their situation was highly regrettable for them as a couple starting out their married life, in that it made their marriage even more difficult that it would have been anyway. Estrangement from their neighbors as well as members of their own family meant that the couple had no one to turn to when they needed help. No one was on their side, so to speak, at least no one dependable, grounded, or consistent who could be turned to as ordinary difficulties arose over the years.

No one from Early's side of the family lived in their vicinity, and no one on Mock's side would have anything to do with either one of them. The level of rejection they had to deal with served to further complicate every problem that came up for them, and, as would be expected, their problems were many and varied. They had to totally get by on their own without any support, advice, or encouragement, which proved to be extremely difficult.

Mock's family never forgave either one of them (especially her) due their belief that the couple's affair had sullied their reputation within the community. For this and other reasons, all of them character-related, members of her family decided not to let Mock or Early's antics complicate their lives any further than they already had. This was one door, they decided, that was going to remain closed. Most residents of the community felt the same way.

Local civic leaders and communal authorities

backed away from the couple as well, believing that more had already been done for them than they deserved. No one, it seems, wanted to become any more involved with the Tigers than they absolutely had to be.

Living with unofficial shunning was not as much of a bother for Early as it was for Mock, due to his preference for living apart from other people. She, on the other hand, did not handle it nearly as well. Whether they liked it or not, from the earliest days of their marriage the two of them had no choice but to struggle to get by on their own.

After the initial anxiety that accompanied their hastily arranged coming together died down, it quickly became clear to Mock that Early's view of their relationship had not budged from what it had been from the beginning. His take on their situation was that he was totally innocent of the accusation of rape that had been leveled against him. Nothing that happened, as far as he was concerned, had been his fault, in that her own behavior had enticed and encouraged him to do what he did.

From his perspective, he had been railroaded into a marriage that he did not want; that he had been linked to someone who thought she was a lot better he was; and that he had been stuck with a woman for whom he did not have even the least amount of personal respect. Through twisted logic that only he could justify, he blamed what happened on Mock, and refused to accept any responsibility whatsoever for having committed a travesty against her.

As far as he was concerned, there had been no justification for forcing him into their so-called marriage, no justification of any kind. The rationale of there being a child who needed to be cared for didn't matter to him in the slightest. That, to his way of thinking, damned well ought to be considered her problem, not his. Anyone, as he saw it, could have been the father of the woman's child.

Mock's family never got past their conviction that she had to have been in some way at least partially responsible for what happened, no matter how vehemently she denied it. They had told her from the beginning not to go to what was likely to become an unruly and out of control stomp in the first place. Having heard rumors and observed incidences of promiscuous behavior on her part on many occasions before the stomp, they thought that in some way she had encouraged bad behavior on Early's part. Because she had shamed their family, they cold-shouldered her from that point on.

Early and Mock were effectively compelled to deal all alone with what members of her own family and residents of the community alike thought of as their transgression, but the burden of doing so fell more upon her than upon Early. The way she was treated amounted to a demonstration not only of the heavy-handedness of the societal strictures of their environment, but also how very little the truth of what happened mattered to those who had tried to help her.

At the time, not too many options were open to

women, especially Indian women, in the kind of predicament Mock got into. When she found herself up
against the wall, she discovered in a hurry that she was
totally out of luck, no matter which way she tried to
turn. Beggars, those who helped her seemed to have
been thinking, had no right to be choosers.

THE BIRTH
OF BONNIE TIGER

WHEN HER DUE DATE finally rolled around, Mock gave birth to a squalling, underweight baby girl. Because Early was not by her side despite the significance of the event, he played no role in the delivery by midwife or subsequent naming of the daughter who was born to him in 1883 when he was forty-three years of age. Mock, who had turned twenty-one not long before, named the baby Bonnie.

Just as the local leaders who pushed Early and Mock into marriage had intended, it was considered a blessing that the baby would have a legal surname at birth. This was a good thing, of course, but a legal nicety was not nearly important enough to overshadow the tragic reality of a child having been born to parents who did not want her or love her in the slightest. Even sadder still was that the baby was unhealthy from the very beginning, and that she remained sickly nearly all the way through childhood, almost as if malevolent forces were already at work against her.

In later years, it was said that those locals who engaged in at least some limited amount of interaction with the family marveled at how Mock had been able to nurse the baby through infancy and raise her up to childhood, in view of the girl's poor health. Too many children did not make it, due to the general state of medical care, not to mention rural medical care, that was available in those days. Even if better care had been readily available, Mock and Early most likely would not have sought it out for their child.

Everyone in the community who understood the basic details of their family situation knew that Early totally ignored his daughter, in the same way they knew he that he treated mother and child alike as if they were dirt beneath his feet. Mock and Bonnie were pitied by one and all, since it was well known that they were living under the thumb of a feckless drunk, a man who provided them with little or no tangible support.

Although the little girl's birth name was Bonnie, she was so cranky and irritable throughout her early years that Mock started referring to her only as "Tiger." It was a nickname that lasted, apparently because most people thought it fit her exceptionally well, even though it was already her surname. From that point forward, most people referred to Bonnie by that single name, Tiger.

NO ONE TO CARE

IN THE TIGER FAMILY'S little corner of the world, few people questioned the right of a husband to discipline a wife as he saw fit, especially one whose wife had reputation as suspect as Mock's. For this reason, Early was free to "correct" his wife in pretty much any way he thought was necessary, and, as the years rolled by, that is exactly what he proceeded to do, with little inhibition or restraint.

It is no overstatement to say that Early was an unapologetic bully as well as an uncaring brute, all rolled into one. Whenever Mock failed to obey any part of what he considered to be his legitimate husbandly demands, he would, in his own words, proceed to "teach her pretty good."

Mock, because she envisioned herself as having no rights to speak of and had no defenders to call on, knew that there was nothing she could do about it. In her context, a woman's personal and social prerogatives were not even remotely close to what they are today, especially in a backwater Indian community like hers. She was up a creek without a paddle, and she knew it.

In truth, Mock acquiesced to and accepted the authority of her husband to treat her the way he did. She was so thoroughly browbeaten that she considered all the awful things that happened to her on a daily as being what she deserved and just the way things are. It was an absolute crying shame that she saw her situation as she did, since doing so had the unintended effect of making it even easier for Early to demean her with impunity.

As the years rolled by, Mock stoically continued to accept her fate, effectively empowering Early to continue to take for granted that he had a perfect right to treat her as brutally and as indifferently as he liked. Their relationship started out that way, and it stayed that way for as long as they were together.

Their sorry household situation was in every sense as miserable for daughter Bonnie as it was for mother Mock. Bonnie, who was now referred to by one and all as Tiger, had no control over the circumstances of her birth, which meant that she had no choice but to grow up in the middle of a domestic relationship so inherently dysfunctional that it would warp her for life. Those who were familiar with her home situation knew her destiny would include an exceedingly miserable childhood.

Throughout her younger years, Tiger had no choice but to watch in tearful silence and quaking fear as her father liberally applied versions of his horse training methods to the development and control of his wife, her mother. There was never any way to tell when he might go off on her. He was a drunken bully, and there was nothing that she, as a child, could do about it. All she could do was get by as best she could, accepting what was happening as a normal part of daily life, something as routine as getting up and getting dressed in the morning.

Due to the increasingly debilitating effects of his unique combination of alcoholism and emotional-mental problems, Early grew even more dissolute and ever more unhinged as years passed by. For Tiger, her home life never got any better than it was at the beginning. Her father's ill-treatment of her mother Mock only worsened, until Tiger began to think of her battering as a normal part of a marital relationship. One of the many great misfortunes of her younger life was that she had no choice but to grow up watching it happen.

MOCK'S DISAPPEARANCE

THE EXACT DATE it happened is unknown, but one day in July of 1891, Etta "Mock" (Burnham) Tiger's years of extreme domestic abuse came to an abrupt and unexpected end. Without warning, she disappeared from the home she had shared for over eight years with her husband Early and daughter Tiger. Her disappearance took place totally out of the blue, with no explanation of any kind. She was there, and then she was not there, and, once she was gone, she was gone for good. From that point forward, not another word was ever heard from her.

At that stage of the episode, though, no one in the community had any idea what had become of Mock. All they knew was that the reality of the awful life she had been living under the thumb of a husband who unapologetically hated her, a man who was a known degenerate as well as a downright alcoholic, might well have made her willing to do almost anything. That reality raised all kinds of suspicion, as would be imagined, right from the beginning.

As would be expected, family members and neighbors put forth a whole raft of theories and offered up all kinds of comments as explanations of why Mock had suddenly disappeared from the face of the earth. Under the circumstances, guess work of this kind had to be expected. It would have been truly unusual if no one had wondered what had become of her.

Rampant speculation is common in situations of this kind. Many plausible explanations put forth to explain her absence, but some of them were clearly more logical than others, which is why all eyes immediately focused on Early. His gruff and straightforward explanation of his wife's absence, bluntly stated, was that she had "Run off and left him with our daughter Bonnie to care for, probably with another man. She'll come back," he predicted, "just as soon as she gets cold and hungry."

It goes without saying that most people doubted Early's assertion from the get-go, mainly because Mock was envisioned as being too browbeaten, mousy, terrorized, and backward to have summoned up enough courage to do anything that bold, even it was fully justified. They knew it was exactly what they would have done if they had found themselves living in her wretched circumstances.

Although unending speculation took place over what may or may not have happened to Mock, neither husband Early nor daughter Bonnie, or Tiger, ever officially reported her missing. Neither did anyone else. Her absence was noted, but it was never reported as a crime, since there was no overt evidence of anything criminal having happened. Normally, a disappearance would have been a matter of grave of concern within the community, but the plain truth was that Mock's absence failed to elicit any appreciable level of "official" discussion. No one took the matter as seriously as was warranted, mainly because her absence really was viewed a likely consequence of yet another domestic blowout within the Tiger household. One crazy thing after another happened out there. If Mock had taken off in search of a new start, then hooray for her, people seemed to have thought. Eventually, folks stopped talking about her absence, as if there had never been a disappearance under highly suspicious circumstances.

When, during the years that followed, the subject of his wife's absence happened to come up, it did so more as a matter of casual speculation than as a topic worthy of substantial discussion or detailed investigation. Even if someone had wanted to pursue the matter, there was no evidence of any kind to be investigated.

Did Crazy Early really do in his wife Mock, as many people suspected? Could he have flown into a rage, beaten her to death, and buried her somewhere out in the woods? It was certainly possible, but it was equally possible that nothing untoward had happened to her at all. No dead body had turned up in the vicinity, and multiple explanations for her absence were equally plausible. As far as most observers were concerned, it would have come as no surprise to hear that the worst thing that could happen, had happened.

But, again, it was not possible to say with certainty what had become of Mock. It was no great leap to believe that she might have deserted their family of her own volition for the very reason that Early had asserted. That she might have done so did not seem in any way far-fetched, not in view of the miserable life she had been living under her husband's roof. Concern over her daughter Tiger would not have been enough to keep Mock at home, since she had never been much closer to Tiger than to Early.

Tiger herself was one of those who had no trouble believing that her mother Mock had run away by choice, due to her up close and personal view of the horrible marital relationship she had had to put with over the years. She readily accepted as gospel truth her father Early's assertion that her mother had, "Run off and abandoned the both of them," probably because she thought that that was a very reasonable path for her to have taken. Tiger lived her life in deathly fear of what her father might do to her if she differed with him in any way. More likely than not, she wished she could have taken off herself, in the same way as her mother.

It did not seem far-fetched to anyone to think that Mock, perhaps after a particularly memorable beating or a turning point when things got so far enough out of hand between Early and her that their marriage became too miserable to tolerate any longer. She might very well have left of her own volition. It was understandable that she might have taken off for points unknown and never looked back. Knowing the Tiger family as well as they did, it was obvious to most of their neighbors that that choice was a distinct possibility.

The sad truth that prevailed during the months and years following Mock's disappearance is that her absence failed to elicit any more than passing levels of concern from anyone. Not a single serious advocate or protector ever came forward to speak for her. Her parents had both passed before she disappeared, but, even if they had not, it is unlikely that they would have spoken up for her, since they had disowned years before. Other members of her family had done the same. Due to her well-deserved nefarious reputation, no one wanted to get involved in any of her affairs.

In the end, what it all came down to is that no one ever considered it their responsibility or made it their business to do any real investigation of what happened to Mock. Most likely, nothing would have come of it, even if they had. She was gone, nothing was ever heard from her, and that's how the matter was left standing.

TIGER'S
HELLISH CHILDHOOD

BONNIE TIGER, who, again, by this point in life was referred to almost exclusively as Tiger, was eight years old when her mother, in the words of her father, "Just took off and abandoned both of us," leaving her fully under the thumb of the one person on earth who was unapologetically hostile to her very existence. Given these circumstances, it was almost inevitable that she would continue to be neglected as a child, and, unluckily for her, that is exactly what happened.

Throughout her tender years, Tiger had no choice but to get by on the lousiest of food, dress in the raggediest of clothing, and generally fend for herself. Her fate was all due to having been rejected by and therefore pretty much ignored by her father Early, who was now her only parent. Saying only that she was "neglected" amounts to understating how very badly she was treated during her years of highest vulnerability. Even a limited level of neglect can have lifelong negative effects on a child, but Tiger's home conditions were much worse than that.

Her father kept her out of school as often as he could, made her feed and care for herself, and, as young as she was, did not hesitate for a moment to use her as a personal servant, terrorizing her all the while. He paid attention to her only when he needed something, or when he thought she behaved in a way that was inappropriate.

Sadly, Tiger had already grown used to being neglected, living with a high level of rejection, and being dealt with like a rag mop. Her mother Mock, before she disappeared, had not been much better as a caregiver than her father Early. Her being left alone with him only upped the ante. The main difference between her mother Mock's parenting behavior and her father Early's was that he thought nothing of terrifying her into absolute obedience, in the same way that he had terrified her mother.

As Tiger grew into her teenage years, it came as no surprise to anyone to learn that Early began to "train" his daughter in the same way that he had trained horses in the past. It was the same way he dealt with her mother and the other two women to whom he had been married. That approach, as far as he was concerned, had worked well with them — at least until, one after the other, each of the damned women parted company with him. In his view, all responsibility for those breakups had been theirs, not his.

Either because he was undaunted by failure or because he was totally incapable of learning from it, his behavior did not change for the better after being abandoned by various women. He continued to handle women his way and his way alone, no matter how badly things turned out.

In Early's social environment, sparing the rod was

seen to be a sure way of spoiling a child, and he whole-heartedly subscribed to this convenient philosophy. Viewing parental responsibility in those terms not only affirmed his own natural inclinations but also provided the few additional degrees of license needed for him to feel free to discipline his daughter in the most deliberate and calculated of ways.

He still resented having been pushed into marrying Tiger's mother, and he resented even more the reality of his having unexpectedly ended up with the sole responsibility for raising a child he continued to insist might not even be his own. He saw his daughter in pretty much the same way that he had seen her mother — that she was a person with low moral standards. Tiger was no more than one more female who would most certainly be susceptible to what he saw as rampant promiscuity in the world around and about them. It was for these reasons that his behavior toward his daughter truly was as mindlessly harsh, illogical, and unfair as it sounds upon explanation.

He was unapologetically determined to steer Tiger away from any kind of wanton behavior, and to do so well before it became too late for meaningful intervention. He was going to make damned sure that she adhered to the high standards of behavior he demanded. He routinely subjected her to punishment so severe that she was terrified to death of him throughout her childhood years. She was as cowed by his presence as all the other creatures he "trained" before her had been, perhaps even more so, since she was only a kid.

If Tiger strayed over one of her father's arbitrarily drawn behavioral lines, she paid a very real price for it. Browbeating, slapping, whipping, denial of necessities, and other unimaginable forms of punishment became a normal part of her daily existence. Some kids live more miserable home lives than normal people can even imagine, and Tiger most definitely was one of them. It was widely known in the area how badly her father treated her, but no one ever said a thing about it. In their context, interfering in another family's internal affairs, except in the most visibly extreme of circumstance, was not done, and most of her abuse took place behind closed doors.

"You are absolutely right to think it was the way her father treated her," some of their neighbors were said to have exclaimed years after the Tiger family's drama was over and done with, "that upbringing caused the girl to grow to be the promiscuous, grasping, manipulative, social climbing schemer she became later in life. What else could have been expected?"

Comments like this were, of course, nothing more than the kind of self-exonerating hindsight that occurs after the worst has already happened. Outcomes are always more apparent after the fact than when problems are taking place. The truth of the matter is that not a single neighbor or relative ever intervened on Tiger's behalf, back when an outside comment of any kind might have been of great relief to her. In real life, that is how situations like hers tend to play out.

When it comes to communal intervention, the

only reality that is worthy of mentioning with respect to Tiger's hellish childhood is that not a single soul ever stepped forward or intervened to help her get by. Worse still, those who were quickest to ridicule or scathingly criticize how she behaved in later years during her struggle toward adulthood were the very ones who had never tried to lift her spirits in any way.

Instead, they condemned and criticized her every action, without ever lifting a finger on her behalf. If she had not helped herself during those early years, Tiger would have had no help at all. She got by, but it was a miracle that she did.

THE DEATH OF EARLY TIGER

TIGER'S SITUATION CHANGED forever in 1904, when her father Early "Hawk" Tiger, the much-reviled husband of her now long absent from the scene mother Etta Jane "Mock" (Burnham) Tiger, died of natural causes at 64 years of age. His sudden passing was not only shocking and disorienting in the way the unexpected loss of a family member usually is, but it was also, as might be imagined, a major turning point in life for his long-suffering daughter.

When Early's body was delivered into the hands of county officials, it was placed in a cheap pine box before his burial in a pauper's grave. His wife Mock, who had disappeared years before, was, of course, not around to witness his service. His daughter Tiger was physically present for the perfunctory graveside ceremony that was conducted for him, but she was not there mentally or emotionally. For her, the whole affair passed by in a blur.

As if the death of her father was not disorienting enough for the girl, his passing brought about a whole new round of local speculation about whether he may have been responsible for her mother's disappearance. The man was dead and gone, but people had never stopped asking if it was not possible that he had done away with her in one way or another, perhaps after having gotten carried away during another of his drunken fits of anger. It was understandable that folks would ponder this question, but those who did always ended up having to settle, in the same way that others had before them, for the same unsatisfying answer: Yes, something of that kind certainly might have happened, but how could it be proven? The possibility of foul play had never been investigated, and now it was too late for the pursuit of meaningful answers.

On the other hand, there were others who unhesitatingly believed that Mock truly did abandon her family, probably, as Early had said, with the intent of starting a new life someplace else — perhaps even, as Early had claimed all along, by running off with another man. They would not have blamed her, not in view of the life she had been living with him.

Speculation about what may or may not have become of Mock was as unchecked as ever, but anyone's guess was no better or worse than anyone else's. For a woman of her time and place, especially one with a child to care for, to have run off would have been unusual, but, in view of Mock's flighty personality and her miserable home environment, it most certainly could have happened. People mentioned again and again that almost any new arrangement she might have come up with would have been a substantial improvement over her life with Early Tiger.

Years before his passing, local authorities had already pigeonholed Early Tiger as, in words they would have used among themselves, "Just another drunken, slovenly Indian." His own insistence on living an indolent, dissolute lifestyle had caused them to take for granted that he would meet a bad end one day, if not for one reason, then for another. The man, in their view, was his own worst enemy.

Considering all the trouble he got into before he died and the criminal record he left behind, it was understandable that authorities and sober-minded residents of the community would have felt the way they did about Early. The only thing that surprised them was that he expired of natural causes when they had taken for granted that his departure would occur in a much more dramatic fashion, such as a shooting or stabbing or some other kind of violent incident.

Before Early's soul left this earth, he had managed to distinguish himself for having been rejected by his fair-weather friends, every member of his own family, and for being abandoned by three wives (two common law and one legal). All had been driven to the point of not being able to stand the sight of him. He had become a villainous figure within his own hometown and was feared and hated by his own daughter due to his having neglected, brutalized, and treated her like a domestic servant. His behavior had been despicable, there was no doubt that. Those who were fully aware of how he emotionally befouled he had become during the last few years of his life conjectured about found it easy to believe that he might even have despised himself.

The description of Early's life story presented in

this narrative is not speculative, since the observations that have been made were confirmed by the man himself. Furthermore, he did so willingly, through providing information for a newspaper article that included key segments about his misadventures over the years.

The article came out during one of his many stays in jail. On the occasion in reference, he was locked up for having beaten up and knifed another Indian during a drunken argument over a comment that was made in the heat of the moment, one that taken as an intolerable slight. The so-called slight was so insignificant that after the combatants sobered up neither one could explain what it was about. Early was locked up anyway since his opponent was physically injured.

The article was written by the female half of the same missionary evangelist couple who had worked with other local leaders to intervene on Etta Burnham's behalf, back when she needed help dealing with the unexpected pregnancy she blamed on Early. Her problem had been solved, as has been explained, by their having railroaded Early into marrying her.

These situations are but two examples of the kinds of problems Early got into over the years, almost always due to habitual drunkenness. For him, strong drink was a perpetual problem, one that that got him into trouble as regularly as clockwork.

The article the lady wrote had to do with the pervasive poverty, alcoholism, and family dysfunctionality that was endemic among the Indians who lived within her and her husband's missionary posting, the very Indians they had moved to the Territory to serve. In it she decried how Indians in general and specific individuals among them were being victimized and unfairly oppressed, and then went on to complain about how conditions among them were worsening rather than improving. She proclaimed that they clearly needed far more help than they were getting.

Her comments had been exactly the kind of thing Early wanted to hear in his predicament, since they helped him identify at least one influential person in the community who might be willing to speak out on behalf of an Indian in as much trouble as he was. He sensed rather than understood the sentiments that motivated her, but he zeroed in on them anyway.

He would have responded in the same way to any angle that might have been of benefit to him during the judicial proceedings that were coming up. Instinctively, he knew that whatever the woman might write would only be of marginal assistance to him, but he figured that even marginal support would be better than nothing. If he could not persuade a person like her to help him get a sympathetic hearing, he surely must have been thinking, then he would not be able to persuade anyone else to do so, either.

Only by happenstance had she and Early come together on this second occasion. In this instance, they unexpectedly came face to face during one of her many visits to the local jail in search of first-person commentaries for the article she was writing. Early spared no effort when it came to playing on her sympathies in any way he could. It worked, too, in that she was greatly saddened, as most anyone would have been, upon hearing his explanation of how Mock had, "Run off and left me to raise our daughter alone."

It seems abundantly clear that Early, who had to have been exceedingly worried about the possibility of having to serve yet another sentence, and due to his many prior offenses, on this occasion perhaps a much lengthier one in the community's bug-ridden, grungy local jail, would take full advantage of the missionary woman's interview. As best he could, he milked the situation for all it was worth. When she finally asked him to explain why he so often found himself in trouble with the law, he realized that it would be a highly advantageous favorable moment to pour out his soul. Without holding back, he proceeded to do exactly that.

He willingly, even eagerly, offered up a litany of complaints about the unfairness of how he had been treated over the years. Because his comments amounted to a veritable case study that would demonstrate the points she already intended to make, their interview worked out even better for her than it did for him.

His willingness to work with her was nothing more than a backdoor effort on his part to mitigate the severity of the punishment about to be meted out for the latest of his many crimes. His comments did not in any way indicate heartfelt sentiment or any change of heart on his part, but that did not seem to be a bother to the woman. To her, interviewing him was more about buttressing the points she was already intent upon making in her article than anything else. To him, it was much mor about eliciting a little sympathy for him personally, anything that might get him off a little easier than was likely to be the case.

"I need to get the hell out of here," he piteously and pointedly exclaimed as the two of them spoke through the bars of his cell. "I need to get back to caring for my daughter. Can't they see that I'm the only one she's got left!" Early spoke freely and expansively in response to any question the woman asked, plainly hoping that whatever she might write might be of some benefit to him during the adjudication of his case.

His lamentations led the good-hearted and well-intentioned woman to include in her article a subseries of comments about how Early's wife, Etta, had abandoned him to run off with another man. In addition, she included comments about the plight of the couple's motherless daughter, who, she took special care to point out, had no one to care for her but her father, a father who, even though he was in jail, still wanted to do whatever he could for his daughter.

And, as luck would have it, it turned out that Early could not have been more correct to think that what the lady wrote might be of some benefit to him. The content and tone of her finished article not only fully described his immediate situation, but also clearly empathized with his plight and, for that matter, pretty much everything else he had had to say. That he was a poor and downtrodden Indian was unquestionable; her article left no doubt about that.

The truth of the situation, of course, was that lady had been in sympathy with Early's plight before he said a single word. Since their arrival in the Territory, she and her husband had been intensely upset over the many problems that plagued the Indians of the region. Misery was rampant among tribal people of the area, and it was concern for the lot of them that that had prompted her to write an article in the first place.

The section of the article that proved to be of greatest assistance to Early was where she repeated his assertion that the man he'd beaten and stabbed had been as falling-down drunk as he was, back when their fight took place. As mutual combatants, either one of them, the lady made a special effort to point out, was equally likely to have been on the receiving end of fist or knife. It would not be at all equitable, she argued, to single Early out for excessive punishment, for no reason other than that he came out ahead in the fight.

If the article did have a beneficial effect as far as Early's situation was concerned, it would be that reading it might at least in some small way may have caused the judge who heard his case to be a smidgen more lenient than he might have been otherwise. He read it, as did most other residents of the area, only a few short weeks before Early's case was adjudicated, so it very well might have had some subtle influence on his decision. That, of course, was all Early could have expected.

It does appear, based on after the fact reading of

court records, that the woman's comments did have at least some beneficial effect from Early's standpoint, since his punishment was not nearly as severe as it could have been. He was sentenced to additional jail time, but perhaps not as much as he might have gotten if the judge had not read the article in advance of the trial.

Looking at Early's situation from a longer-termed perspective, it really didn't matter much that he might have been sentenced to a shorter period behind bars in this one situation. Immediately after he was released from jail, he dove headlong right back into the same dissolute lifestyle he had been living before the fight. Even after receiving a break, he found it impossible to muster enough self-control to derive any real long-term benefit from what the lady had to say about his life situation.

Early's personal story was only one small part of the moralistic diatribe the lady wrote in hope of generating additional public support for uneducated and impoverished Indian people in their region. Although she described their plight as being very grim, her commentary, if anything, understated the severity of the problems that arrayed against the tribal people of their area. That economic conditions were tough in the Territory in those days was a reality no one disputed.

Her comments stimulated a good deal of discussion when it was reprinted in various local church newsletters after it appeared in regional newspapers, but after an initial polite expression of interest it ended up at rest on a back shelf alongside many other studies of its kind. When writers delved into problems among the Indians in her day, this is what typically happened.

It was so patently obvious that conditions among the Indians were deplorable that people considered the matter a truism, something that no one could do anything about. Problems among them were so extensive that no one could envision how they might be solved. Putting a simple bandage on them, they figured, had not helped in the past, which meant to them that doing more of the same would produce no better results. Most non-Indian residents of the Territory reasoned, "What is the point of writing more articles about conditions that are already obvious?" Doing so, in their view, was more like beating a dead horse than doing something productive. It would not help, in other words, to keep restating what was already known.

Early's small part in her article was forgotten after only a little while. Most likely, the majority of those who read it most like stopped thinking about him as soon as they learned he was still in lockup, which was, as far as they were concerned, exactly where he deserved to be. He had, as they all knew, admitted his guilt, and in his setting an Indian, or, for that matter, anyone else who committed a violent crime, usually did not elicit much public sympathy.

The kind-hearted woman's story, in other words, did not stimulate anything close to the level of constructive thought or action that would have been required to help Indian people in any meaningful way. Like other commentaries of its kind, it drifted off into historical oblivion, leaving conditions among the Indians exactly like they were. At the time, it was difficult for people to envision how any truly progressive solutions could have been put in place.

One point worthy of repeating before the subject of Early's passing is, pardon the expression, laid to rest, is that even in the remote section of the country where he lived, there remained folks who claimed that he was no more than another victim of his time, one more hapless Indian brought low due to circumstances he could not control. He grew up among whipped and demoralized people, they contended, so why was it considered a surprise that he ended up becoming a whipped and beaten man? "The circumstances of his life," they argued, "were what led to his making as many mistakes as he had over the years. Any one of us might have done the same things, had we had grown up the way he did. Why, then, judge him so harshly?"

Hearing bits and snatches of this kind of speculation about her parents' flaws and misbehavior had long since become a normal part of Tiger's daily life. As Mock and Early's only child, it was an environmental reality, something that never, ever went away, no matter how much she wished it would.

Discussion of these sensitive topics eventually became so perversive that they took place whether Tiger heard them or not. People blathered on whenever, wherever, and any way they pleased, without giving a thought to what a devastating impact their comments might have on a young girl growing up. Her parents were denigrated at will, whether doing so had an adverse effect on her or not. Talk of this kind was a constant in her life; it never went away, and runaway gossip on the part of neighbors and townspeople, in precisely the way that the more sober-minded residents of the community thought it might, ended up having a terribly adverse effect on her self-esteem.

Shortly after Early was buried, it finally occurred to a few his neighbors that his passing had created a need for a shift of attention away from the problems of the Tiger household as they had existed in the past and towards the matter of checking on the welfare of his now twenty-year-old daughter, Tiger. With her father dead and her mother, if not also dead, at least no longer on the scene, she was the only surviving member of what was now universally considered to have been a hopelessly misguided family. Now that the worst had happened to the girl, neighbors began to wonder what kind of intervention, if any, might be needed on Tiger's behalf. Their belated concern was a clear-cut case of too little, too late, but Tiger, as one might imagine, and as it happened, had by that point begun to wonder the same thing herself.

TIGER'S
RELEASE FROM PURGATORY

EARLY TIGER'S SUDDEN DEMISE came as no great surprise to any local authority figure who had had to deal with the negative effects of his drunken, always-in-trouble behavior over the years, but his passing was an absolute shock for his browbeaten, exceedingly forlorn daughter Bonnie, who was known to one and all by her nickname, Tiger. The only thing that surprised the solid citizens of their community was that Early had not met the kind of violent end his lifestyle invited.

Tiger, on the other hand, was rattled to the core by the loss of her father. She had been so immersed in the oppressive task of getting by from day to day under his tyrannical thumb that the possibility of something of such magnitude of his dying had never so much as crossed her mind.

Like so many who are confronted with the reality of having to deal with the unexpected sudden loss of a close family member, Tiger had a great deal of trouble believing that her father really was dead and gone. Observers saw her bewilderment as one symptom of the normal bereavement people go through upon the loss of a loved one, but it was not. In truth, her reaction was anything but normal bereavement, in that all she really felt was an enormous sense of relief, which, of course, was not even close to what anyone would call a normal reaction.

Tiger's initial response to news of her father's death was to withdraw into a state of disbelief, a period of wonderment over how such all-powerful force in her life could have disappeared in what seemed like no more than an instant. He had been the dominant force in her life for so long that it was nearly inconceivable that he would not be around to persecute her any longer.

His passing occurred so unexpectedly that for a while she was unable to mentally process that something that profound had taken place. It seemed impossible. His domineering presence had been the worst aspect of her existence for as long as she had been alive. His awful behavior had been the worst aspect of her life, worse, for example, than seasonal heat or cold or mosquitoes or hunger in the pit of her stomach. Various forms of discomfort and privation had been part and parcel of her daily existence for as long as she could remember. Left shocked and reeling in the wake the event, she struggled to wrap her mind around the reality of it. Could it actually be true, she wondered in amazement, that his malevolent presence was no longer around to make my life miserable?

Tiger's unspoken fear was that her father's passing was a merciless joke someone was playing on her, and that somehow or another he might pop up and begin persecuting her all over again. He was like that, she thought to herself. On numerous occasions, he had demonstrated that he was hateful enough to do things that spiteful, if only for the sake of making her life a little more miserable than it already was. Nothing, as far as she was concerned, was impossible when it came to him — not even resurrection.

Due to what can only be described as residual fear of her father's potential for malevolence, Tiger's initial reaction to his death was a whole lot different from how she came to feel about it a short while later. A lifetime of negative conditioning can have that kind of effect on a person, and that's exactly the kind of effect it had on her. She was about as browbeaten as a young person could possibly be.

Initially, she was unable to envision any other approach to life than to keep on keeping on, right where she was. Almost by rote, she thought her only option was to continue living in the same way she and her father had in the past, plodding along at the homestead as she had when she was fully under his control. Having been kept out of school and raised as much apart from the community as her father could manage, the life of an isolated and impoverished Indian was all she knew.

All she could imagine was carrying on as she had in the past, almost as if her father had never left. She would have to do what had to be done to get by off the ragged property the two of them had lived on since the day she was born. Sameness, in other words, was her only expectation. Because she saw no other option, she chose to continue living in familiar isolation — even though their old place always had been and still was more of a prison than an actual home. Tiger had been released from purgatory, but she did not realize it, not just yet.

FROM INTRANSIGENCE TO LOCAL MORALITY TALE

THE STORY OF HOW Etta Jane Burnham as an unmarried woman had flagrantly disobeyed the wishes of her parents, insisted on attending a forbidden stomp, ended up being pushed into a loveless marriage, and then vanished from the face of the earth was told and retold throughout her family's region of the Territory. It was a tale too salacious to be ignored, so talk of her misadventure took off like a house afire. Parents, for example, took special note of how obstinacy, truculence, and disobedience on her part had led to her own come-uppance.

Her story was embellished in new and creative ways with nearly every retelling, until, after innumerable iterations, it morphed into a full-fledged morality tale. It was a local event parents of all stripes and colors could trot out when they needed help keeping their kids under control. "Do as we tell you," they'd say, "or you'll wind up like that silly girl, Mock."

Mock's escapade became one of those stories that, as the phenomenon is described, "grew legs of its own." In the end, folks in general, and particularly parents, began to think of what happened to her as a significant regional happening, primarily due to its solid utilitarian value.

Mock's misfortune provided a perfect case in point for parents to bring up when they needed to make it perfectly clear to their kids that they ought to toe the lines set out for them. Better still, it had happened right in their own backyard. It could not have been any clearer that Mock's own duplicity before, during, and after the ill-fated stomp brought about most of the major problems she experienced thereafter. Her own behavior paved the way for the assault that occurred that night, which, in turn, led to the miserable marriage she was pushed into. Many parents concluded no other story could be more instructive than that of Mock.

Stories like Mock's circulate in small communities like theirs because those who live in such areas are rarely in much of a hurry. Besides, living in isolated rural location creates a need for people to talk, or gossip, to stay in contact — more so, even, than many of them are willing to acknowledge. Whether they admit to it or not, many of them welcome any opportunity that comes up to interact with their neighbors.

The upright, ordinary folks who live in small communities typically do not mind if large parts of their personal lives are open books, mostly because they don't have much of anything to hide. For this reason, they don't think of open discussion as being much of a problem. This innocent reality is why shooting the breeze — or, as some would put it, gossiping — so often becomes a staple. It is a predictable aspect of rural existence that takes place anywhere and everywhere. In the immediate community, for example, one such place was the local post office.

Located in a corner of one of three general stores in town, the post office was one of those places that sooner or later every resident had to visit. When they picked up their mail, almost all of them would do a little shopping in the store as well — sometimes, in fact, all their shopping. Neighbors interacted with one another as they dealt with these activities, and as they did, it was common for them to chatter like magpies.

Unexpectedly passing by a neighbor in a small town often takes on greater significance than such a happening truly warrants, all because it creates a good opportunity to visit and catch up on things. On many occasions, interactions of this kind became more like a mini-social event or special happening than something purely functional. Such things tend to go this way, in places that are populated mostly by hard-working farmers.

In warmer weather, people spoke of Mock as folks sat on chairs and benches positioned near the front steps of the store. In cooler weather, they talked about it as that sat on seats among the collection of chairs and benches that were available aside the tall wood stove located within the store. The seating, as well as the stove, had been put in place by the store owner, whose goal was to keep folks on site until they had spent as much money as they could be induced to spend. Patrons were aware of why these comforts had been put in place, but they appreciated the owner's thoughtfulness, anyway. He knew as well as they did that there was little choice but for them to visit his store, whether he offered any comforts or not.

Neighbors talked freely about Mock's parents, unreservedly and at length, whether they knew what they were talking about or not. All sorts of real and imaginary possibilities were put forth to embellish what they truly knew about them, and there was always a lot of speculation about what may or may not have become of Mock. Folks took for granted that they had a perfect right to sound off about her parents in any way they desired, paying no attention to speak of to the effects their comments had on the unfortunate couple's child.

It was in these ordinary settings that innocent discussions sometimes became truly hurtful; and it was in such settings that permanent damage was done to Tiger's fragile psyche. Whenever her mother Etta Tiger's story came up, neighbors would blare on about it in any way they wanted to, whether Tiger could hear them or not. Things she did not hear firsthand eventually got back to her, anyway. In a small hometown like hers, not much of anything remained secret. Tiger heard all there was to hear about her parents' mistakes, whether she wanted to or not.

It was in this way that the impact of Mock's youthful display of willful defiance fell as much or more on her daughter Tiger as it did on herself. Mock's suffering took place between the date of her marriage to Early and the date of her disappearance, but Tiger's period of suffering most likely lasted from the date of her birth until the date of her death. After she disappeared,

Mock was no longer around to suffer the consequences of her own bad behavior. That role, unfortunately, fell squarely upon the slender shoulders of her highly troubled daughter, Tiger.

Throughout the most formative years of her life, Bonnie Tiger had no choice but to put up with blaring, opinionated, condemnatory references to how her mother had so obstinately insisted upon attending that miserable stomp. It never ceased. Constant criticism of her mother's ignominious behavior was all Bonnie, aka Tiger, ever heard. There was no end to it, it seemed; and, because she had to contend with these conditions as she grew up, there was no way she could avoid feeling beaten down herself. She had not done anything wrong, but it was almost inevitable that she would begin to feel as if she had.

Tiger had no choice but to grow up as a second, or even third-class citizen, a tainted person within her small hometown. It was an environmental reality that made her advancement as a teenager into young adulthood even more graceless and painful than those years already are for most young people. To her, it seemed like some sort of evil plan had been put in place, for no reason other than to make her situation even more unbearable. On many occasions growing up, had she known of a hole big enough for her to crawl into, that's exactly what she would have done.

MOCK'S
STORY FADES AWAY

EVEN AT A YOUNG AGE, Tiger's most fervent wish had been that all discussion of her mother's misbehavior would die out altogether and never brought up again. In view of her situation, it could not have happened soon enough. Regrettably for her, though, that's not how things went, not even close. The very opposite is what really took place, in that talk of Mock's misadventure not only increased, but also took on a whole new life of its own. Much to her chagrin, nearly every resident of their region of the Territory had heard all about it.

Because it was titillating as well as helpful, the story held up for years before interest in it finally began to wane. It took a lot of years for the novelty of it to wear off, more than long enough for loose talk to cause a great deal of psychic damage to the girl on the receiving end of it, and Mock and Early's daughter Tiger was already a very fragile person. No one set out to hurt her, but her neighbors behaved in ways that did exactly that.

Eventually, though, interest in Mock's story, as would be expected, finally did begin to fade away. It happened gradually, in coincidence with the way life began to change in rural towns throughout the country. Her community was only one of thousands of small farm communities much like it that were hard hit by the advent of the tractor agriculture. It brought about great changes in farming, which led to people worrying about matters a lot more important than local gossip.

The advent of tractor agriculture had a devastating effect on small-scale farming operations. Seemingly overnight, the family farms that had been what rural life was all about were no longer economically viable, leaving many families caught up in a struggle to make a living.

Tiger's community was also further set back than most small towns by the economic decline that took place during the hard years of the Dust Bowl and The Great Depression. These two overlapping occurrences caused additional economic devastation in the region around where it was located.

Due to the economic decline, local farms, which for years had prospered in the agricultural land around her community, and had been the backbone of its existence, struggled on for a while, but then finally failed. When they did, the merchants that served them also went into the red and, eventually, they, too, went out of business. This was followed by the failure of the town's two banks.

Local economic conditions worsened until more and more residents awoke to the realization that no choice was open to them but to move to larger cities, or even out of state, to earn a livelihood. When the economy continued to decline, more and more people had to face the same dark choice; either move on or do without.

Most of them, as would be imagined, chose to move on.

As more and more families moved away, the doors of first the high school and then later the grade school were closed. Boarded up homes and business were readily visible. More quickly than any of the locals would have imagined possible only a few years earlier, not a single commercial enterprise, and only a few civic offices, remained standing in the small community. It had always been a relatively small and isolated place, but it now looked like something of a ghost town.

Then, when conditions sunk to such a low point that no further public services could be provided, the distressingly small handful of residents who remained in the vicinity decided that they had no choice but to dissolve the township as a functioning municipality. A few years after this decisive step was taken, the small town that had been taken for granted as having a promising future was reduced to little more than a scattered collection of rural households.

Eventually, after the changes that have been described, only a few stalwart elders remained in the vicinity who even remembered there had been a young woman by the name of Mock — a woman who disappeared under suspicious circumstances after having flagrantly disobeyed the parents who loved her. Her story no longer commanded the attention it had some years before, primarily because those elders who still lived in the area had far more important things on their minds.

Most of them were no longer much interested in

local gossip, since they, like everyone else, were occupied with the more practical matter of figuring out how to get by during the worst economic downturn anyone could remember. Even those seniors who did recall Mock's story, the folks to whom it had once been an extremely hot topic, realized that they had much weightier issues to deal with, whereupon Mock's escapade was relegated to the backs of their minds.

Soon, only a small number of people could recall what had happened to the luckless twosome, Mock and Early Tiger. These folks passed on to their kids what they could remember of the affair, but they, too, in short order, soon became seniors themselves. After a few decades, only a few older folks remained who could recall what had happened to the couple, and most of them did not remember the story very well.

As the local economic decline continued, almost all of those who could remember what happened to Mock had no choice but to move away, typically to live with and be cared for by their children or to reside in senior residences in larger towns within Oklahoma or in other states. Time and tide wait for no man, which means that people did what they had to do to get by, whether they really wanted to make changes or not. Getting old is not easy for anyone, no matter who they are or where they live.

Because the economic decline proved to be unrelenting, more and more people left the community and the broader general area for greener pastures. Many of the homes in town, even those that were still usable and livable, ended up being abandoned, due to there being no one around to rent or buy them. Salvaging them was not worth the labor and expense that kind of effort required, which led to many of them eventually falling in on themselves and rotting in place. Others were destroyed by fire, and still others were wiped off the map by one or the other of the severe storms or tornados that are so common in the state of Oklahoma.

Conditions continued to deteriorate until, finally, not much of the little community remained to be seen. By the time the 1980s rolled around, most first-time passers-by could not even tell that a small town had ever existed at the site.

By this point, of course, Mock's story, for all intents and purposes, had been all but forgotten. Only a few people could remember much about it, and those who did had scattered to new locations within Oklahoma or other states, where they lived with relatives or in senior residences of various kinds. From the day of her disappearance, not another word was ever heard from or about Mock, the young woman whose brazen disobedience once created an absolute tempest.

*****

COAL MINING IN THE INDIAN TERRITORY

IN THE UNITED STATES during the last half of the 1900s, projects were launched throughout the country to clean up abandoned and hazardous mine sites, typically for the purpose of reclaiming land for ordinary productive purposes. These efforts were accelerated during the 1970s, when a federal law known as the Surface Mining Control and Reclamation Act was enacted. The new law had a direct impact on the State of Oklahoma, because there were many such sites out in what used to be referred to as the Oklahoma Indian Territory.

Commercial mining of coal in the Territory got underway as far back as 1872, back when railroad companies first began extending lines into the region. As early as 1883, at least six railroads were operating coal companies in the Territory, and as soon as they got more lines in place, they quickly became the dominant competitors within the Territorial coal industry, although many small companies were in operation as well. Even before Oklahoma became a state of the union in 1907, a well-developed railroad network and coal industry was in place throughout the Territory.

Coal mining as an industry grew at a rapid pace well into the 1890s. Many small-scale independent miners were doing business right alongside the huge railroad-associated mining companies that had come to prominence. Coal mining remained a growth industry through the 1920s, when a downturn began that continued off and on all the way up to the beginning of World War II. The downturn was severe enough to force a high number of once-thriving coal companies, large and small alike, to shut down their operations altogether.

Today, closure planning is required in advance of launching a new mining venture, but pre-planning of this kind was not required during the boom days of the early coal industry. For economic reasons, early mining companies often did not take adequate steps — or, in some cases, any steps at all — to ensure that closures were safe, much less environmentally protective. This was especially true in remote areas, such as, for example, the Oklahoma Indian Territory.

In many cases, mines that played out were walked away from and abandoned, leaving behind many acres of mined land that were not reclaimed for safe and productive use. This, of course, became a major problem over the years, one that cried out for public policy attention. Abandoned surface and underground mine sites became the source of a whole raft of hazardous conditions. These situations led to enough injuries, accidents, deaths, and environmental disasters to make the question of how to deal with mined land, which had not been reclaimed, an even greater public concern.

For this reason, a new and more sustained effort

to deal with these problems was launched in the 1970s in an effort known as the Surface Mining Control and Reclamation Act. The act established a trust fund through a coal tax to provide the wherewithal necessary to reclaim abandoned coal mined land, which posed a danger to public health or safety. In the 1980s, authority for administering Oklahoma's Abandoned Mine Land Reclamation Program was turned over to the Oklahoma Conservation Commission. After this was done, the responsibility for helping the commission identify those sites that posed the greatest danger to public safety was assigned to local conservation districts.

The local conservation districts used U.S. Geological Survey maps to identify those sites most in need of being cleaned up. Removal of obvious hazards such as open mine shafts, dangerous high walls, and toxic water bodies was assigned the highest priority. Reclamation efforts were concentrated on sites next to roads and highways, especially in populated areas.

Environmental remediation at the sites to be reclaimed could involve activities such as the removal of pollution or contaminants from environmental media such as soil, groundwater, sediment, or surface water. If nearby properties were found to have been contaminated through decades of emissions to soil, groundwater, and air, even more expensive remediation could be required. Mine ceiling dust, topsoil, surface water, and ground water on abandoned sites — as well as on nearby properties — was required, both before and after any remediation effort.

Because these remedial activities could be extremely costly, individual property owners could not afford to pay for them by themselves. It was for this reason that some level of public engagement had to be involved before any remediation would take place at many hazardous sites. Individuals who owned property on which the most hazardous sites were located had to worry about the adverse effects of they had on their property titles, even if they had not caused the problem. An encumbrance of this kind, of course, could adversely affect the value of their land.

Among the many property owners in Oklahoma who owned land on which an old mine site was located was an Okmulgee County resident by the name of Allen Owens, who, after he became aware of reclamation efforts being afoot, pursued with great diligence any opportunity he could identify to clear up these problems on his own place.

The abandoned mine located on Owens' property had been shut down many years earlier, back when the seams of coal it was placed in service to exploit were extracted. When this happened, the investors who owned the operation pulled out any of their equipment and machinery that could be used elsewhere or sold for scrap. They also laid off their remaining employees and moved to a new location.

Back when the company was closed, the land on which the mine was located was too remote and sparsely populated for the owners to feel any great need to worry much about cleanup in the interest of public safety. In those days, no one expected an outfit that went under to do any more cleanup than necessary, and, back then, that was not very much.

The only effort the departing mine owners made in the interest of site safety was to install a sturdy barbed wire fence around the clearly hazardous open shaft they left behind. The fencing was installed more to prevent grazing cattle from bumbling into the pit than to protect the safety of any unwary people who might, by chance, wander through there on the way to someplace else. Except for this token effort, the coal company did nothing else to clean up after themselves. They simply abandoned the site and drove off, leaving behind a mess, which from that point forward remained a safety hazard, an eyesore, and a public nuisance.

After the closure, ownership of the land on which the site was located changed hands multiple times. New owners accepted the old mine sites as a given, something they did not even think of doing anything about. Even if they had wanted a cleanup, they could not have afforded to do one. In their day, nothing of the kind was expected of them, anyway.

Back when the mine was in operation, there had been no reason not to pile tailings in any location that was convenient. Now, though, many years after the mine's closure, the acreage selected for these deposits became a prime location for future development. The piles were located right between the mine pit, supporting buildings, and railroad spur, and the county road that ran along the north side of Owens' 80-acre ranch.

It had become obvious that the strip, if not for the piles of tailings, would be a highly marketable piece of land.

Owens' place was located roughly eight miles southwest of the City of Henryetta, immediately off the Okmulgee county road and the rail line that went by the now long defunct rural Okmulgee County small farm town site of Bryant. As a property owner, Owens wanted nothing more than for the acreage on which the tailing had been piled to be leveled and turned into lots that could be put up for sale. He was fully aware of the market potential of this part of his ranch. The land was thought to be an ideal location on which to build what were referred to as "ranchette-style" homes — ones much like the dwelling Owens lived in himself. There was land enough for a string of them.

Owens worked in an office in Henryetta, but he earned a little extra income each year by running a small herd of beef cattle on his ranch. He kept up a herd more to justify his ownership of the ranch than because he earned much from the effort, but he spoke glowingly of the operation anyway. He encouraged every person he met to call him "Al," and he had become locally well known for extolling to anyone who would listen the virtues of, "living out in the country" like he did. That he promoted this point of view in his own economic interest was also well known.

It was well known that Owens' motivation for wanting the old mine site on his place cleaned up and returned to productive use had everything to do with the possibility of getting his lots to market and little or nothing to do with concerns such as clearing up an eyesore, protecting cattle, or assuring the safety of the few people who might ever have a reason to trespass across his land. Despite his obvious self-interest, most residents of Henryetta as well as local political leaders still favored clearing up the visual blight of the old buildings and mounds of pilings out on his place. The old mine site had been an eyesore for so long that most people did not want to look at any longer.

DIAMONDS SHINING BRIGHT

IN RECENT YEARS, Allen "Al" Owens had taken pains to point out that the site had become more dangerous than ever, since many of the posts that had been put in place to hold up a barbed wire fence around the open shaft had rotted away at their bases. For Owens, keeping his cattle from stumbling into the pit had become an ever-increasing concern. In several places, strands of wire affixed to the posts had pulled loose and were sagging down, nearly to the point of touching the ground. Left as it was, the site was obviously dangerous, but even at the risk of losing an occasional steer, Owens was secretly glad to leave it as it was for a while. Any form of hazard that bolstered his case for a cleanup of the site was alright with him.

Of greatest interest to Owens was a provision saying that for projects approved at his location or anyone else's, owners would not have to pay much out of their own pockets for the work to be done. Way back when land reclamation funding first became available through grants to the state government for projects of this kind, he had been astute enough to complain about his situation. The mess on his land was a hazard as well as an eyesore that needed to be cleaned up right away, he claimed.

Local officials eventually agreed, even though

other Okmulgee County sites were more hazardous, polluted, or toxic than his and therefore ought to have been assigned a higher priority. Owens knew as well as they did that this was so, but that had not prevented him from pressing his case and applying for help anyway. To his surprise, his project had been approved, probably due more to the need to complete a few small but highly visible seed projects than to the merits of his application.

Because the Owens site was not contaminated with toxins or other pollutants that might damage the air or water, it was clear that a low-tech solution would suffice as an approach cleaning up the mess out there. No more would be required than removing all safety hazards associated with the open shaft, knocking down and burning the abandoned buildings, removing the eyesore caused by the piles of tailings, and leveling off and over seeding the land to make it attractive for higher uses, uses such as housing. This view of his project, it goes without saying, was music to the owner's ears.

Just as soon as the project was approved, the county issued a call for bids to get the cleanup under way. Rock Solid Excavating of Tulsa, a regionally well-known contractor in that line of work, submitted the low bid for the job, and, after their bid was accepted, not too long thereafter the day and hour rolled around for the company to get down to work.

It was for this very purpose that that on an early morning in the spring of 1985, four dusty and much-used pickup trucks showed up out at the old mine site on Owens' place. The four drivers parked their trucks beside three bulldozers that had been unloaded there late the previous late afternoon. The dozers were parked right next to the fence around the open mine shaft, which was itself close to the various run-down and ragged service buildings that were to be demolished. The men were ready to get to their assigned tasks. For each of them, it was the beginning of another ordinary eight hours of work.

Three of the four men — Dave Hixon, Pete Cellier, and Bobby Wilson — were heavy equipment operators, guys whose job it was to buck the dozers that had been brought in for the project. The fourth man, Bill Presser, who was their supervisor, was there for the purpose of verifying that each member of the crew had shown up fit and ready for work, assuring the readiness of the equipment that that had been brought in for their use, and clarifying and fleshing out each man's assignment for the day. The world over, that's what foremen do.

In addition to these fundamental duties, Presser was also responsible for doing whatever could be done to make sure the men paid proper attention to operational safety after they got to work. Rock Solid was a stickler for work site safety, which meant that, along with providing oversight and support for crews at the locations that were assigned to him, as a foreman for the company he was expected to assure exactly that.

The job of foremen such as Bill was to rotate between job sites like the present one, clarifying each man's duties for their day of work. The crewmen knew that at this job site their overall task was to return to productive use the acreage on which the old mine was situated. Their work was to begin with infilling the primary vertical mine shaft, off which various lateral shafts had been spun off to reach the underground seams of coal that originally justified the mine's existence. They were to fill the vertical pit, ignoring all the stopes.

The contract also called for the crew to push down and burn or bury all the dilapidated wooden buildings, ramps, and elevators that were still standing; collect and pile up any metal that could be salvaged for scrap; level out the huge piles of tailings that were built up while the mine was in operation; and, after these steps were completed, to smooth off and overplant the whole site. As far as the men knew, the whole purpose of their work was to make sure the land was safe for livestock grazing, which was the current major use of the acreage around and about the mine. They did not know and really did not care to know about any other uses to which the land might be put.

Historical facts having to do past practices within the coal mining industry out in the Indian Territory were irrelevant to the guys who showed up to work at the old mine site that morning. Their job was to clean the place up, not to ruminate over how it got to be the way it was or how it might be used after their work was done. To them, the cleanup was no more than another entry on a long list of similar jobs they had worked together on over the years. The four men were good friends as well as long-term coworkers, which meant that they knew one another exceptionally well. They expected to be at the site for as it took to get the job done, and then to move on to yet another.

Their standard operating procedure before starting work each day was to touch bases with one another by means of an early morning tailgate briefing that was delivered by their supervisor. So, after parking their trucks, opening their doors, and stepping out of their respective vehicles, they ambled around to the back of the one that belonged to Bill, who was their supervisor.

Yawning, stretching, and scratching their necks and bellies as they sipped coffee out of thermoses, they patiently watched and waited as Bill set up for the delivery of their routine morning briefing. They did the same thing to kick off every shift, as a means of making sure they were all on the same page before they got rolling.

Bill typically began by spelling out daily assignments for each one of his direct reports, which meant that this was a step the guys took for granted. In addition, they knew he had to talk about the proper maintenance and care of the equipment that was there for their use. That, too, they took for granted. Finally, because their company, Rock Solid Excavating, had a reputation for being a stickler for worksite safety, they knew Bill would have to deal with that topic as well.

Stressing the need for safety was standard practice in their line of work, even though, as far as the guys were concerned, Bill's doing so would be more of a formality that anything else, since there was not much that could be said to them that they had not heard a hundred times before. Same old, same old, they were thinking to themselves, assuming that this was going to be another ordinary work shift. But, due to a string of events that could not have been anticipated and that could not be repeated in a hundred years of trying, they could not have been any more mistaken.

That morning, Bill had a lot more in mind for the crew than a typical tailgate briefing. There was something special he wanted to share with the guys under his supervision, something he could hardly wait to get to. He and his men were more than mere workmates, they were good friends as well, guys who had known one another for years.

With a lopsided grin on his face, he dropped the tailgate of his pickup, jumped up to get seated on it, and began setting out the same manila pocket folder of job-related materials he regularly had on hand for their morning briefings. The men had learned that Bill was nothing if not a competent and well-organized supervisor, and one of the many things they knew about him was that he started his briefings the same way whenever they had one.

It was for this reason that on that morning the men could not help but notice how in addition to putting out the manila folder and other job-related materials they normally saw, Bill set out an additional item they had never seen before — a fancy-looking black bag, a drawstring affair made of some sort of velvety material. For them to see something of that kind at a job site was unusual, especially during one of Bill's briefings. He was a by the book supervisor, which meant that he was not in the habit of bringing anything personal or unusual to a work site.

Before their boss said a single word, the men knew that something out the ordinary was about to happen. The manila folder and other job materials were familiar, but the fancy-looking black bag certainly was not. It drew their attention like a magnet, in the very way that Bill had known all along it would. He had set it out for that specific purpose.

Once Bill saw that the men were focused in on the flashy black bag, he knew he had their undivided attention. It was obvious that he had something special to say, and the way he put out the bag had made it equally obvious that he could hardly wait to get down to it. It was obvious that he was in a great mood, too.

"Guys," he said, grinning from ear to ear, "I have somethin' I want to show you. After three years of goin' together, me and Betty have agreed that we ought to consider tying the knot and making it official. We're all together on that, and I've told her I'll be back in Tulsa this weekend to ask her a formal question.

"She said she can hardly wait to hear from me because I know she knows exactly what I'm going to ask, but I promise you, she's going to be more pleased than she can imagine when she hears it. Even if I do say so myself, the ring I'm gonna offer her is as impressive as one can be. In this case, my saying so isn't conceited or showin' off, since I didn't go out and buy it myself.

"I'm going to offer her a family heirloom, a piece of jewelry that's worth over $10,000, accordin' to some of the people who know about these things. You see, right after I told my mom that we're serious about settling down, she took off her own ring and gave it to me to give to Betty. It was her own wedding ring, the one my dad gave to her. Now that he's gone, she wants Betty to have it, although she's worn it since the back when she and my dad got married.

"'This is going to be your third go at it,' she said to me when we talked, 'and this time around, Bill, honey, I really want to see it last. It'll please me very much for Betty to have my ring,'" she said, "'since what I want more than anything else is for you to marry a woman who's mature enough for the two of you to stay together from now on.'

"'Your first marriage failed because you and your wife were way too young to get married in the first place, and your second one fell apart because you got married on the rebound. Don't deny it,'" she told me, "'because I know you like a book. We all know you did exactly that. You never did love that woman.'

"'What I want,'" she said, "'is for you and Betty to have a marriage like your father and I had, one that will last for as long as ours did — over 55 years. Taking off my ring and giving it to you is the best thing I know to do to show how much I want the two of you to be happy.'

"'Your happiness means the world to me,' she said, "'but only if you to settle down and stay together from now on. Your two divorces have been even harder on me than they've been on you, and I don't think I could handle another one. Take the ring with my blessing, but you've got to promise me that you're going to put your heart and soul into making a go of it.'"

"And you know," said Bill, who had gotten caught up in the spirit of the moment and turned a little misty-eyed in a way he had not intended, "that's exactly what I intend to do. No matter what happens, there's not going to be any turning back. Come hell or high water, I'm gonna make sure this one works out. Her givin' me that ring meant the world to me. Mom is as right as rain about how miserable it is for a marriage to fall apart. I've learned that as well as anyone, so, once we're married, I'm going to do whatever I can to make sure I never hear the word divorce again!"

After he poured out the words he had on his mind, Bill reached out to pick up what the guys now recognized to be a well-made, personally monogrammed jeweler's cloth bag. Pulling open the drawstring, he withdrew yet another attractively finished item, in this instance an elaborate flip-top jewelry box. It was obvious that the box, too, was another custom effort, since it was made of some of rock-heavy, pearly black material not typically used for containers of its kind. Into the base section of the interior of the box, a single slit had been cut, and, in the slot, Bill's mother's beautiful diamond ring mounted on a gleaming silver wedding band had been inserted.

Upon opening the box that had been specifically designed to showcase it, he proceeded to show off the precious bestowal his mother passed on to him to offer to Betty, smiling large and wide all the while. Against the deep black background of the container, the glittering array of smaller diamonds seated around one larger diamond and inserted in a gleaming silver setting made the ring sparkle like a star on a dark night. The ring would have stood out in any form of illumination, but it was especially beautiful that sunny early summer morning.

The guys didn't know a thing about fine jewelry, but no special knowledge was required for them to realize that they were looking at a gorgeous and expensive wedding ring. On the other hand, they knew Bill's girl Betty very well, and only one good look at the ring was more than enough for them to see that she would most likely slip a gear when it was offered to her. That it would hit her where it mattered was unquestionable; the guys saw that in an instant.

The guys thought it was an especially good thing that Betty was sure to be pleased with the ring, since they liked Betty as much as they liked Bill. All of them were close friends, and they couldn't have been happier for Bill and Betty alike. The two of them did indeed seem to make a great couple.

In the very best of moods, Bill urged each man to

take a good, close look at the spectacular ring. "Take it out of the box," he said, "and hold it up to see how it gleams in the sunlight. It's a real a beauty," he gushed, beaming nearly as brightly as the ring itself. "No wonder mom has always been so taken by it. Betty's gonna love it, too; you can bet your next paycheck on that."

Doing exactly what Bill encouraged them to do, the men began the process of passing the ring from one to another, making sure not to rush the process. Being very deliberate, each man took it out of the slot in the box, held it up to the light, and echoed Bill's comments about how attractive it was. One after another, they confirmed how right Bill was in saying Betty was going to love it. Any woman would, they agreed, not because it was expensive, but because it had genuine family significance and was truly beautiful. "There's no way you're going to go wrong with this ring," one of the men assured Bill, speaking for the other two.

"Yeah," he agreed; "It really is special. Dad sure did it up right for Mom, back when they were young. When I had it resized, I had all aspects of it checked out and made sure the big and small diamonds and their settings were cleaned and polished. After 40 years of wear, it needed a little sprucing up. The case it's sittin' in," he repeated, "I had custom made. I couldn't be any more pleased by how the whole package turned out."

Without a doubt, the ring his mother handed over to him to offer to Betty was one that any woman would be pleased to wear. What made things even better was that her gift amounted to an expression of confidence that his latest marriage was going to last for a lifetime. His mother liked Betty, and Betty liked his mother. His mother's sense of confidence about their pending union was even more buoying that the ring itself. Like his mom, that, more than anything, was exactly what Bill wanted and needed.

Then, shortly after the heavy black box in which the ring was mounted was passed to Bobby Wilson, the youngest member of the crew, an event occurred that in no more than a few minutes thereafter Bill would begin to think of as a happening straight out of hell. The disaster began when the mobile field phone in his truck started ringing off the hook.

To take the call, Bill excused himself with a "be right back." He slipped down from the tailgate on which he had been sitting, and then walked around to the driver's side of his truck. An upper-level manager at the head office in Tulsa was on the line, all steamed up over an issue that had cropped up at one of the other job sites under Bill's supervision. Because the crew up there was waiting to get to work, resolving the problem could not be put off. It might be necessary to drive all the way up there, he realized, even before the briefing he was in the middle of could be completed.

It was aggravating that his special moment with the immediate crew had been interrupted, but he knew he had no choice but to tune them out for a while. Because he had been hired for the express purpose of putting out fires of the kind the call was about, he muttered, cursing under his breath, "Well, hell; if that's what I need to do, then that's what I've got to do, since that's what I'm here for."

"This is gonna take a while," he said, turning his head back toward the three men he had not finished briefing. He called out over his shoulder as he was walking away, hoping to make sure they could hear him a little better, saying "You guys know what needs to be done, so go ahead and get to work. We'll finish talking after I get this mess sorted out."

"Bobby," he continued, "you start by pushing down the perimeter fence around the mine shaft and knocking down some of the old sheds, but first take a good look at the ring. There's no hurry, so don't rush checking it out. When you're finished with it, put the bag on the front seat of my truck." Bill was so pleased with the ring that he wanted each man on the crew to take as long as he wanted to look it over thoroughly.

After that, Bill walked away from where he and the men were standing, hoping that he and his counterpart would be able work out a solution for the problem without his having to make a trip up there. At this point, he was still oblivious to how far south his workday was about to go.

His problem began when Bobby did not clearly hear what he was told to do with the ring after he finished checking it out. It was not surprising that he didn't, since Bill made his comments while he was distracted, speaking over his shoulder, and turning to walk away from the men. Not a one of them heard him distinctly, least of all Bobby. All the guys picked up on was a garbled message, something along the lines of: "You guys know what to do, so get on to work while I deal with this situation. We'll finish your briefing later." With these comments, Bill thought he had covered his bases, but he most definitely had not.

So, when Bobby finished admiring the ring, he returned it to the slot in the heavy black box that had been cut for it, placed the box on top of the flashy black drawstring bag, and set both items on top of the rear track of his dozer. His dozer was parked right beside the driver's side door of Bill's truck, leaving the bag in a position so visible that it would be impossible for him not to see it when he returned.

Bobby thought Bill would return in no more than a few minutes to collect the ring, as soon as he finished his call but certainly well before the men polished off their coffee and got to work. He said he would be right back, and he had placed the box in a position so visible that it could not possibly be missed. This guileless assumption became the first of several mistakes Bobby Wilson made that shift, errors of judgment that quickly turned it into one of the very worst days of his young life.

When his partners Dave and Pete climbed aboard their dozers to start work after finishing their morning coffee, Bobby absent-mindedly climbed aboard his own dozer as well. His doing so was an unthinkingly automatic reaction, caused by their unstated practice of starting out each workday in pretty much the same way.

When the senior men boarded their machines to get after it, Bobby, because he was junior and had been conditioned to do so, immediately fell in behind them, without even giving it a thought.

Completely forgetting that he left Bill's precious ring on the rear track of one side of his dozer, he did not think of it again until the rear tracks of his powerful machine rolled forward enough to reach where the front tracks had been a little while before. He did not even as much as look in the direction of it until a few seconds before he saw the heavy black box tip forward from its location on top of the velvety black bag, fall between his tracks and blade, slowly tumble down the weather-worn gradual slope at the top of the open pit, and fall off into the abyss.

In a heartbeat, one of the most pleasant mornings on the job he had ever experienced turned into a moment more dismal than any he could imagine, short of being crushed to death after rolling his own dozer. Cursing himself with a vengeance, he could not believe he had allowed such a stupid thing to happen. His boss, he knew, was going to have an absolute fit about it. Would he be fired? he wondered. Yes, he thought to himself, he would be fired; there was no doubt about it.

Why, he asked himself, do crazy as hell things like this always happen to me? Sick at heart and literally shaking in his boots, he knew he had no choice but to tell Bill what had become of the priceless piece of heirloom jewelry he intended to present to Betty that very weekend.

As soon as Bill returned to his truck after working out a solution for the problem up in Tulsa, Bobby proceeded to tell him exactly what had happened. In the blunt, ham-handed way the other two guys on the crew knew to be characteristic of him, he artlessly explained what had become of the precious ring, apologizing profusely as each word was uttered. Would it be possible, Bobby wondered to himself as he spoke, for a man to be any more miserable than he was at this precise moment?

As he expected would be the case, his boss most definitely did not take the news well. Bill, in fact, after Bobby finished telling him what happened, could hardly believe his ears. He visibly blanched as white as a sheet, turned wobbly at the knees, and then flushed beet red in the face. Was it even possible, he thought to himself, that a member of my own crew, one of my own good friends, could have allowed something so damned dumb to take place?

He knew his mother's ring was irreplaceable, in the same way that he knew that Betty and she would be literally sick over the loss of it; there was no doubt about that. Why, he asked himself, as Bobby had asked himself only a few minutes earlier, do crazy as hell things like this always happen to me? His mom and Betty would surely hold him responsible, no matter how the ring happened to be lost. Thinking about it, his stomach rolled and rumbled as if he had eaten a very bad meal.

Then, in less than a heartbeat, Bill's anguish

flared into unthinking outright anger, whereupon he turned with eyes ablaze toward the currently dejectedly miserable junior equipment operator who had been irresponsible enough to leave the damned ring on the tracks of a dozer and then gone off and forgotten it. Glaring at him in a way that made the young crewman cringe, he tore into Bobby as if he had thrown the ring into the pit on purpose.

"You knew how much that damned thing meant to me, and bless her heart, to my mother, and you also knew how much it would mean to Betty," he snarled, "so how in the hell is it possible that you could have been so damned careless and forgetful? Why in the hell didn't you put it on the front seat of my truck like I told you to? Would that have been so damned difficult? What kind of idiot would leave something so precious on the tracks of his dozer, then go start the damned thing up? If I could get away with it," he bellowed, "I'd throw your sorry ass down that damned pit right behind it!"

By this point Dave and Pete had noticed from the seats of their dozers that an altercation of some sort was taking place between Bobby and Bill. They turned off their machines and returned to see what the fussing and cursing was all about.

Upon hearing what had happened, they, too, found it hard to believe that the precious ring had been lost. Their buddy Bob, they saw in an instant, was truly in a world of hurt. They knew how much that ring meant to Bill and his mother.

One of many things the men liked about Bill as a supervisor was that he always remained calm and collected, even in the face of all the crazy kinds of problems that tended to come up in their line of work. There was always something, but Bill had been a boss who seldom lost his cool over anything.

Now, though, here he was, ranting and raving like a mad man and swearing like a drunken sailor. They had never seen him so upset. They found it understandable that he was angry, but they still felt sorry for Bobby, whose hide was being scorched in a way that he had never experienced.

After fuming and cursing and berating him for what to Bobby seemed like hours on end, Bill turned toward the younger man and said: "I don't have a choice but to get that ring back, and you, by God, are gonna be the one who goes down in that pit to get it. You'll get down there and find it, or you damned well won't have a job out here to worry about. You lost the damned thing, and you're damned well gonna be the one who goes down there and gets it back!"

"I can't go down in that hole," Bobby groaned in response, who had immediately realized that he was going to have to do exactly that, whether he liked it or not. The whole idea of going down in the hole unnerved him. "The sides of the pit are so old and crumbly they could cave in at any minute!" Going down into that dark place was the very last thing he wanted to do, but he knew he was going to have to do it, anyway.

"That pit's been there for a hundred years and it

hasn't caved in yet," Bill barked in reply, "even though it sits beside a railroad and a county road that carry big loads right by again and again every day. That's been goin' on forever. If it was gonna cave in, it would have done it back when you were in short pants. Besides," he snarled, "if it does cave in, it would damned well serve you right!"

When Dave and Pete heard Bill utter those words, they knew there was no way their foreman was not going do everything in his power to retrieve the ring. Bobby, they concluded, was up a creek on this one. He would have to correct his own clumsy mistake, because there was no way under the sun that Bill was going to leave that ring down there where it was.

THE RECLAMATION PROJECT
THAT BEAT ALL!

ALL FOUR OF THE MEN knew that retrieving the ring was going to be a hundredfold more difficult than railing about how it had been lost. It was clear to each of them that getting it back was going to be a real challenge.

Getting down into the pit would be as difficult as it would be dangerous and finding the ring even if someone did get down there would be even more difficult still. The hole was over 120 feet deep, and there was at least five feet of standing water at the bottom of it. From the top, there was no way to tell how many feet of decaying plant matter or other kinds of debris had blown or been thrown into the pit over the years. There was certain to be a lot of muck, but what lay below the water level would not be known until someone stepped off into it.

Going down into the old mine shaft would be dangerous, there was no doubt about that. Be that as it may, Dave and Pete knew there was nothing they could do for Bobby, nothing other than cringing over what lay in store for him. There was no way to get him off the hook. Bill had decided what had to be done, and all they could do was try to help him figure out how to go about doing it.

Once the question of figuring out how to retrieve

the ring became the focus of attention, Bill calmed down somewhat. Because he was a task-oriented person, he quickly regained the highly objective composure that was one of his most notable characteristics. As if a switch had flipped in his head, he reverted to his normal self and began to dig in on solving the problem at hand.

Lost in thought and without offering a word of explanation, he turned away from the crew and walked back over to his truck. Thinking that their boss was still in a stew and might fly into yet another fit of rage at any moment, the men looked on as he sat in the seat of his truck with a pad on his lap, watching as he became lost in thought. The guys were afraid to make a peep, due to how fearful they were of getting him riled up all over again.

Seated there in the front seat of his truck, Bill doodled on a yellow tablet as he tried to come up with an approach to retrieving the priceless ring. Furiously scribbling away for as long as it took, an idea finally took shape. When he stepped back out of the truck, he had a sketch of a solution in hand. It was a simple and straightforward plan of action, but it was one he thought more likely than not would work.

After explaining what he wanted to do, he asked the men if they would be willing to help him retrieve the heirloom ring that meant so much to his family. The men not only agreed but also promised to work without pay until the job was done. On top of that, they offer to work more unpaid hours to make up for the contractual hour that would be lost while the search was underway.

It was clear to them that only by finding the ring would Bobby ever get back on good terms with Bill, who, despite his calm exterior, was still extremely upset and extremely worried. The possibility of restoring a tranquil workplace, they figured, was well worth putting in a reasonable amount of unpaid effort. Getting things back on an even keel was exactly what the guys were in the market for.

After the men agreed to do what they could to help, Bill placed their contract work on hold for the duration of the recovery effort. Now that they were down to brass tacks, he began lining out responsibilities for each member of the crew. After he did so, a flurry of activity that lasted for days got under way.

Their work began with dropping a weighted line down into the pit to determine exactly how much standing water there was at the bottom of it. With that information in hand, Bill sent one member of the crew to Henryetta to rent a gas-powered portable water pump and bring back a whole batch of miscellaneous supplies. His list included three five-gallon cans of fuel, four 50-foot by one-inch ordinary garden hoses, eight sheets of one-inch plywood, a strong pulley, two dozen top-grade 2 X 4s, 15 yards of hog wire, a large box of four-inch drywall screws, a package of wire staples, three ordinary hinges, and an old-fashioned door clasp.

While one member of the crew was away securing the supplies, another used a dozer to knock down an old ramp that stood alongside the railroad spur that ran by the mine. From the wreckage, the men pulled out two

6 X 6 timbers that had rotted out at the base but were still solid enough to be placed four feet apart as bars across the open mineshaft. When the plywood sheets arrived, they were secured to the cross bars to create a sturdy platform across the pit.

Once the platform was in place, they erected a sturdy frame structure over space that had been left open above the center of the open shaft. Across the top of the frame, they rigged in a heavy metal cross bar. Then, the pulley was mounted beneath the cross bar. For enough strong cabling to reach the bottom of the pit, winch cables at the front of two of the three cats were bolted together to create one single long band.

The 2 X 4 studs, hinges, and latch were used to construct an elevator-like 4 X 4 X 8-foot cage that could be lowered down into the pit. For protection against any loose rock that might fall as it was lowered and raised, they covered the cage and cage door with a double layer of hog wire.

When the jerry-rigged platform, housing structure, and cage and pulley system were ready for use, they draped the lengthened cable that had been extracted from the winches on their dozers through the pulley mechanism on the housing frame and bolted one end of it around the entire cage. From then on, lowering or raising the cage became a simple matter of driving the dozer backward or forward.

While these tasks were under way, the one-inch hoses Bill ordered had been linked and then lowered down to the bottom of the shaft. Using the rented gas-powered pump, standing water was drawn out of the pit and funneled off to a depression low enough and far enough away to keep it from draining back into the pit. After the water was pumped out of the pit, all that remained at the bottom was an undeterminable level of muck and debris.

With the winching mechanism in place and the standing water pumped out of the pit, their next step was to lower Bobby down to the bottom so that he could begin to search for the ring. His unenviable task was to do the dirty work of scrounging through filth until it was rooted out. They knew it was down there somewhere, buried in the pool of slimy muck.

Whether he was ready or not, the hour had finally arrived for Bobby to redeem himself. So, down he went, off into the deep, dark hole, wearing only his normal clothing, a pair of duck hunter's hip waders, a lighted miner's hardhat, and holding an ordinary garden rake and hoe for use as tools. It goes without saying that the recovery effort was anything but a high-tech operation.

After a descent that went off without a hitch, the cage hit the bottom of the shaft. When Bobby opened the hog wire-covered door, he stepped off into two-to-three feet of slime and rotted plant matter and other debris that stunk so bad he could hardly stand it.

"It stinks like a sewer down here," he shouted to the men above. Trying to breathe through his mouth instead of his nose, he began raking through the slime in search of the black box. Bill and the men thought the box would be located very quickly, since the pit, although it was deep, was only about 14-foot square. That, though, was not even close to how things worked out, due to a turn of events that not only caught all four men flatfooted but also knocked them back on their heels for a while.

What happened was that with nearly every pull of the rake, Bobby hit something solid. He pulled up more scattered pieces of rock than anything else, but lots of bones were drug up as well, mostly the remains of animals that had fallen into the pit — some of them, unluckily for Bobby, much too recently. Their decaying carcasses along with all the rotting plant matter down there explained why the pit stunk as badly as it did. It was obvious that many unwary animals had fallen into the pit over the years and had either been killed by their fall or starved to death in a hopeless struggle to get back out. Bobby realized that that had to be why the place was so revoltingly foul.

"There's dead animals all over down here," he complained, although he knew he wouldn't get much sympathy from above, "and the stink is bad enough to gag a maggot. Wading through all these putrid old bones is nauseating and creepy as hell." The guys would not have argued with him about that, but they knew Bobby's only option was to labor on until the ring was found.

"You didn't give me no choice but to come down here", Bobby shouted bitterly to Bill and the other two men up above, "but I sure as hell don't have to pretend that I like it." Bitching and moaning all the while, he continued the dirty, sickening work he could not get out of doing. Saying that he wasn't happy amounts to describing his attitude in the mildest possible terms.

Then, with his next pass of the rake after making the most recent of his long stream of complaints, he pulled up yet another piece of bone. In this instance, though, it did not look like any of the others he had seen. After shaking off more of the muck in which it was covered, he realized to his horror that what he held in his hands was a human jawbone. After disgustedly throwing the bone aside, he raked a little more in the same location. Before long, he found himself looking right down into what was clearly the open eye sockets of a human skull.

There was no doubt about it, he realized in an instant; he had to be standing literally right in the middle of the skeleton of a human being. Already unnerved by all the old bones he had turned up, a fleeting image of his having accidentally fallen into an open grave struck him like a hammer.

Just as soon as that awful thought flashed through his mind, he reacted by yelling at the top of his lungs to the men up above, "Get me the hell out of this hole right now and call the cops. There's a dead body down here!"

As quickly as the crew could make it happen, they drew Bobby up and out of the pit. Noticeably more than a little rattled, all he was able to do for a while after reaching the top was keep repeating what he had already said.

"Are you sure?" Bill, Dave, and Pete asked in unison. "With all the animal remains you've been seeing, is it possible that you mistook an animal jawbone for one from a human being?"

"I'm damned sure," he replied: "I know enough to recognize a human jaw with teeth stickin' out of it when I see one. There's no doubt about it," he declared; "I saw what I saw, and what I saw was part of the skeleton of a human body. Believe me," he promised, "there's a dead man down there, maybe even several of them."

Once they took Bobby's story to heart, Bill placed a call to the Henryetta Police Department. As soon as the police had a good understanding of what they were being called upon to investigate, they called in the city's fire and rescue personnel to follow them out to the mine site. Within 20 minutes, five different emergency vehicles were parked beside the open mine shaft and within a few more minutes, the entire site was cordoned off as a crime scene.

Specialists in the form of first the police and then search and rescue people and finally staff out of the county coroner's office took over the crime scene from that point forward. They began with a preliminary investigation for the purpose of determining what, exactly, had taken place out at the mine. Bill and his men were told to stand by until the investigators were free to take more information from them.

The police used the winch and cage system Bill

and his crew had put in place to conduct their initial search of the pit. It worked so well that the search and rescue team used it after that. Because it was already in place, their system was used for the entire duration of the investigation and subsequent recovery effort.

"The contraption you guys came up with," they told Bill and his team, "is whole lot safer than some of the riggings we end up working with. If it ain't broke," they said, "why fix it?" The guys really liked hearing that, simply because it meant that their own effort was not going to be wasted. On the contrary, their work proved to be more helpful than any of them imagined it would be.

Investigators used their jerry-rigged lift to haul up barrels of muck until the pit was emptied down to a solid bottom. As the barrels were brought up, every ounce of content was sifted through a screen in search of evidence of a crime having been committed.

Most of the bones that were recovered were those of coyotes, foxes, possums, cows, and other animals that had fallen into the pit over the years, but not all of them. And, sure enough, as Bobby had said would be the case, the complete skeleton of a human being was discovered as well.

In the end, only one item of hard evidence was discovered that had any connection to the desiccated and plainly very old skeleton that was brought up out of the pit, but it was more than enough to lead to a positive identification of the body. The recovered item was a metal belt buckle, on the back of which, after lots of scouring and cleaning, the roughly inscribed name of Etta Burnham was still legible. Initially, this was puzzling, since no one by that name had been reported missing.

It was impossible to immediately determine how long the body had lain in the pit, but deterioration made it clear that the bones had been there for many years. Oily, tarry residue that had collected at the bottom had been helpful in terms of preserving bones and buckle alike; it left them in better condition than they would have been otherwise.

Upon confirming that the skeleton was that of a female, investigators researched old records until they made a positive identification. With certainty, the body was that of Etta (Burnham) Tiger, who, it seemed reasonable to assume, had most likely been at the bottom of the hole since the date of her disappearance, way back in 1891.

A peripheral but vital and wonderful benefit of the search and recovery effort out at the old mine shaft, at least as far as Bill Presser and his three crew members were concerned, was that Bill's priceless heirloom ring was recovered during the investigative process. It turned up as the muck from the bottom of the shaft was screened for evidence.

Dave, Pete and, of course, Bobby most of all, were as pleased as Bill was by this turn of events, since finding the ring put Bobby back in Bill's good graces. That their former harmonious working relationship was restored an enormous relief to all four men. For Bobby, losing the ring had led to one of the wildest rides in what for him up to that point had been a notably low-keyed work life. In the future, he swore to himself, he was going to be a hell of a lot more careful about everything he did than he had ever been in the past.

*****

AFTER BILL CLEANED UP and repackaged the precious ring, he placed it in Betty's hands and asked her to marry him, as he had intended all along. Betty, on her part, was as even more delighted with the ring than Bill thought she would be, and the two of them went on to get married as planned.

Bill's mother was as pleased as Betty and Bill by how things turned out, mainly because she felt certain that her twice-divorced son was finally on the right track and that through giving the couple her treasured ring she had had some influence in terms of helping them get off to a positive start in a marriage that was going to last.

Dave, Pete, and Bobby were minor celebrities among the scores of guests who attended Bill and Betty's wedding. Why wouldn't the guys have been pleased and excited, considering the series of human-interest articles that appeared in local newspapers explaining not only how the fabulous wedding ring was lost and then retrieved but also how the remains of a missing person had been discovered during the recovery process? It had been a truly remarkable happening, and those who attended the wedding got a real kick out of being a small part of it.

The three crewmen, in particular, were as pleased as punch by how their efforts out at the mine site had led to the discovery of the ring and, much to their surprise, helped solve a long-standing missing person case as well. It amazed them to think that if an accident as random as Bobby's having accidentally dumped Bill's ring into the pit had not happened, the body of the Okmulgee County woman who had been missing for 94 years would never have been recovered. Bobby had been only a few minutes away from beginning to fill in the pit, and, if he had had even started, much less completed, the one task, the woman's whereabouts would have remained a perpetual mystery.

After talking over what happened until they totally exhausted the topic, the crewmen concluded that Bill and Betty ought to think of the incident as a little special icing on their wedding cake. In their view, losing and then recovering the ring ought to be taken as a good omen for the couple, an indication that their marriage was going to be a good one, one that was going to last for as long as they lived. That, they pointed out, was what Bill and Betty said they wanted, and what happened should be interpreted as a sign that that was exactly how things were going to work out.

Everything that had taken place, as far as the three crewmen were concerned, warranted being thought in the best of terms, as something that was meant to be. Others who were there felt pretty much the same way. A detective who worked on the case and was invited to the wedding summed up the whole incident as well as anyone could have when he said: "Well, hell; don't it just beat all!"

A RECOVERY
WITHOUT CLOSURE

BY THE SLENDEREST of slender threads and in a next to impossible way, the whereabouts of Etta Jane (Burnham) Tiger had finally been discovered. It happened due to a random chain of events that in a million years could never be repeated.

Among the law enforcement officials, search and recovery specialists, forensics examiners, and others who conducted the recovery effort, it was considered a near miracle that Mock's body had been discovered. To them, retrieving the lost ring was nothing more than a side event, but solving the decades-old mystery of a woman's disappearance was truly remarkable. Even those who did not believe in miracles fully agreed on how amazing it was that such an unlikely series of events had taken place.

Despite the sentiments of the moment, by no stretch of the imagination could the woman's body having been found be described as a great outcome, since nothing more of her was recovered than a collection of skeletonized remains. In terms of learning how the poor lady got where she was, discovering her body did not help at all in terms of figuring out how she got down to where she was found. That, of course, was what inquiring minds wanted to know: How in the world did she get down there in the first place?

The discovery of Mock's body led to all kinds of speculation about what happened to her, but that was about all it did. Finding her remains was of no help in terms of explaining how her demise came about. When details about her relationship with Early were brought to light, that information added even more fuel to an already brightly burning fire.

Just as they had shortly after her disappearance, people wondered if her sorry excuse for a husband murdered her and thrown her lifeless body down into the pit, in the very way many, according to their research, had suspected from the moment they learned she was missing? That seemed to be the most likely of all possible explanations, since the husbands of missing women, especially those husbands who are known for drunkenness and violence, are always prime suspects.

The problem, though, just as it had been at the time, was how to go about proving it, especially if an accusation must be proven beyond any shadow of doubt. That, of course, was the crux of the matter. Despite what lots of people thought, there was no clear-cut way of unequivocally documenting Early's involvement.

It was also clearly possible, as it had been from the beginning, that Mock may well have been murdered by someone else, or, for that matter, that she may not have been murdered at all. Abductions and murders were not unheard of in her day, any more than they are in any other, and it was also conceivable that she might have committed suicide by throwing herself into the pit. Due to the miserable existence she had to bear at home, she had as much reason to take that desperate and forlorn desperate path as others had before her. It was in no way unthinkable that a person as miserable as Mock might have considered suicide an easy way out. Some did that kind of thing to themselves in her day, and for the same reasons, as some do in ours. It has been that way for as long as there have been troubled people.

In the end, those who pondered the question of what happened to Mock always arrived at the same conclusion, which was that any entry on the list of conceivable explanations of how and why she ended up in the pit was as plausible as any other, especially in view of her wretched marital relationship with Early. Misery had been part and parcel of the poor woman's daily life.

Even if there had been a way of proving that Early murdered Mock and hid her in the mine shaft, it would have been impossible to bring him to justice. There is no way, sorry to say, to punish a dead man for his crimes. If Early did do in Mock, he got away with a cold-hearted murder.

Even though finding Mock's body did not lead to what anybody would have described as a satisfactory or positive end, knowing what happened to her did bring about at least some level of closure. Even that, as far as those who dealt with the recovery were concerned, was a lot better than never learning what became of the poor woman. Even a limited degree of certainty about what became of her was, in the opinion of authorities, preferable to a disappearance remaining on the books. In a case like hers, members of the local powers that be said among themselves, authorities ought to be thankful for any kind of information they got for a case of its kind. In many such situations, no information of any kind is ever turned up.

Once Mock's identity was confirmed, it was relatively easy to find out that she had had a husband and a daughter, but, since the two of them were already dead, the information was not helpful in terms of determining how to deal with her remains. Various members of her extended family were contacted before articles about the recovery appeared in regional newspapers, but that effort proved to be of no help, either. No one wanted to get involved in her situation, thus no one showed up or could be located to claim her body.

Although some members of her family would have read some of the many articles that written out about the discovery of her body, again, not a one of them stepped forward to say a word. Why would they, in view of her behavior in the past?? In the years before her disappearance, she had done as much as she could to burn as many family bridges as possible. From those days forward, she had had no real relationship with anyone in her family, and, when news of her having been found under such suspicious and awful circumstances began to circulate, no one wanted to deal with such a repugnant situation. Their reaction — or, rather, lack thereof — had the effect of adding a whole new layer of sadness to a story that was already pitiable enough.

Who in their right mind, her relatives seemed to have concluded, would want to get involved in Mock's affairs at that late date, especially when her situation might very well turn out to involve a case of cold-blooded murder? Besides, the incident occurred several generations in the past, so why would any of them want to get involved now? They knew next to nothing about Mock, anyway. It was, they evidently figured, the county's role to deal with her situation.

That is exactly what happened. County officials took over from that point on. Standard practice in cases of un-mourned deaths like Mock's was for the practical matter of dealing with unclaimed remains to default into the hands of officials of the county in which the death occurred. And this was what happened in her forlorn and depressing situation. Because the County of Okmulgee officials had no other option, they dealt with her in the way that is customary in situations like hers.

Her remains were placed in a cheap casket, the casket was buried in a pauper's grave, and the gravesite was topped off with a small metal cross with her name and the pertinent dates stamped on it. They dealt with her, in other words, in the same way they did with her husband Early, back when he, too, died a pauper's death. These desultory steps ought to have brought an end to the wretched story of Mock's Bad Stomp, but they most definitely did not. In some ways, in fact, the story had only just begun.

THE PAINFUL LEGACY
OF MOCK'S BAD STOMP

ETTA JANE "MOCK" (BURNHAM) TIGER left no tangible property behind when she was buried in a pauper's grave. That, regrettably, is how it goes for destitute people, irrespective of where or how they meet their end. Mock's only true legacy was her hapless daughter Bonnie, or Tiger, who was as forlorn as she was due to her local reputation having been cast in stone even before she got out of the chute. For mother and daughter alike, Mock's insistence on attending that accursed stomp had truly awful consequences.

While she was still an innocent child, no resident of the community was able to look in Tiger's direction without thinking about what had happened to her mother Mock. All of them knew her story, and practically to a person they took for granted that her daughter was destined to have to deal with a whole raft of personal problems later in life, especially after she grew old enough to head out on her own. That, people thought to themselves, is the effect a pair of unfit parents typically have on a child.

"The apple," her neighbors avowed to one another, most likely, one would suspect, nodding sagely as they spoke, "never falls far from the tree," belying the exact mindset that caused them to assume that a bad outcome for the girl was a foregone conclusion. Her neighbors pigeonholed Tiger from the beginning, and then treated her accordingly, as if her course in life was irretrievably set.

Some of the more fair-minded residents of her hometown realized how the unstated pressure of so many people seeing the girl's future in such a negative light could create a self-fulfilling prophesy, which would most definitely not be good for her. Still, there were too few who thought that way to make an appreciable difference. Tiger had to deal with condescending neighbors no matter which way she turned, which really was, of course, in every sense as demoralizing as the more thoughtful members of the community thought it might be.

It was totally unfair that Tiger had to deal with preconceived attitudes no matter which way she turned, but she had to live with it all the same. In their little fishbowl of a town, her neighbors' negative views were impossible to escape, and their way of thinking created a heavy cross for a young girl to have to bear. She had no choice but to live with the way her neighbors had her labeled, whether she wanted to or not.

Her father Early's unforgivable offense against her mother Mock had been the major cause of most of the diffuse as well as direct agonies of Tiger's young life, but it was not the only one: disobedient, disrespectful, and inexplicably obnoxious behavior on the part of her mother was yet another, since that was what caused her to go to the stomp in the first place. Although Tiger was not responsible for either problem, the great challenge of her life was that she had to deal with their aftereffects, anyway — whether she wanted to or not.

As if the short-term consequences of her parents' indiscretions were not already bad enough, their behavior had negative consequences that extended far past Tiger's immediate situation. It did not end with making her daily life an ongoing headache — not by a long shot. The ripple effects of it created problems for many years thereafter, some that spanned multiple generations.

In the heat of the moment, the highly paternalistic pressure that community leaders orchestrated and brought to bear on Early and Mock as a means of pushing them into getting married was thought to be the only viable way of dealing with the problem at hand. Most of those who were involved thought it was for the best, without giving much thought to long term implications. They had the best of intentions, but in real life good intentions do not always lead to the kind of positive results that are hoped for or expected.

In Mock's case, a high-minded solution, in and of itself, did not come remotely close to assuring the kind of happy outcome its promulgators hoped to see. The agonizing awfulness of the resultant marriage was proof in spades of this being so.

Unsparingly but truthfully described, Tiger's parents' marital relationship was a disaster from the beginning, absolutely and unequivocally. It was so disastrous, in fact, that the adverse effects of it reverberated down the family line for generations and led to more misery than in their worst dreams any of those who tried to help the couple would have imagined possible.

Some marriages evolve into outright hells on earth, and Mock and Early Tiger's was one of them. An abundance of empirical evidence exists to show how in a situation like theirs a vicious circle can be created — one where one bad outcome leads to yet another, until things get so totally out of hand as to be irredeemable. That is exactly what happened in Mock and Early's case.

As the misery of their marriage dragged along, problem after problem cropped up — problems that neither of them had enough desire or wherewithal to contain. Well-adjusted people do not like to even hear of, much less to think seriously about, marriages that are as wretched as the Tigers', but what happened is what happened. There is no after the fact way to describe it as anything other than exactly what it was. Their marriage, in a nutshell, was bad enough to serve as a textbook example of how unspeakably harsh and how terribly brutal the business of getting along in the world can become, especially for an immature person like Mock, who, despite her attitude and practiced obnoxiousness, was relatively young and innocent before she got into it.

No serious parent needs to be told that a single poorly-thought-out decision made by a child during its years of youthful innocence can do great damage to that child's prospects in life, since they know it instinctively. It is for this very reason that dutiful parents spend all kinds of effort cautioning their kids against all the many perils that may confront them as they bumble toward adulthood. Mock's parents Andy and Ruby, for example, had done all they knew how to do to keep their daughter on a straight and narrow path, but, in the end, all their efforts were in vain. Their child, for whatever her reasons, they so painfully learned, simply did not want to be helped, and it is impossible to help a person who does not want any help.

It was sad enough in itself that Mock's young life spiraled out of control following her association with and subsequent marriage to Early Tiger, but what makes her story even more tragic is that her only true legacy, her daughter, Tiger, had to pay a terrible price for her intransigence as well. It is painful as well as sobering to come face to face with the reality that one human tragedy often begets more of the same, but that very thing is more common in real life than people of good faith like to think. The truth of the matter is that it happens all the time.

In terms of Tiger's future, her mother Mock's personal tragedy provides an illustration of how great truth resides in the often-repeated observation that the impact of an emotionally meaningful experience, whether good or bad, never fully goes away. Instead, it is embedded deep within in the psyche, and one of the great challenges of human existence is that we must learn how to manage our own memories. If we do not do this well, remembrances of highly impactful experiences can pop up unexpectedly, occasionally right in the middle of contending with the ordinary demands of daily life. Whether we recognize it or not, experiences we like to think of as having been put behind us can be a major source of the subconscious thoughts and feelings that guide our daily decisions.

Living a successful and happy life, in other words, is far more dependent than most of us realize on how effectively memories of the past are managed. When our mistakes and negative shortcomings are kept in proper perspective, a solid base on which to build a good life is the result; when they are not, we can become our own worst enemies. Some may consider this observation too obvious to deserve stating, but it is not; instead, it is important enough to warrant constant mindfulness. For many if not most people, some of the most significant problems of the moment really do originate with their problems of the past, and in many situations, personal behavior is not nearly as rational as we like to think it is.

It seems clear from reading between lines that this kind of thinking was a problem throughout Mock's life and, perhaps even more so, during that of her misguided daughter, Tiger. In terms of how they coped with life, it seems that they got into a rut, and, once they became entrenched in that self-created rut, they could never muster enough wherewithal to drag themselves out of it.

Those who understood how Early Tiger truly felt about his responsibilities as a husband and father knew why the only care he provided for his wife and daughter,

Mock and Tiger, was what others shamed him into providing. He resented having to deal with either one of them; and that was the reality of their situation. It was for this reason that he never did anything more than the basic minimum for either one of them. He horribly neglected and abused his wife and daughter alike, much more that anyone ever realized. Even worse for Tiger was that her mother, in terms of providing basic care for her child, had not been any more diligent than her husband.

When Mock was still at home and then even more so after her disappearance, her daughter Tiger had had no choice but to effectively raise herself. Appalling conditions lead to appalling results, which are the inevitable consequence of childhood neglect. Tiger's childhood experience was more miserable than any young person should have to endure.

Given the utterly wretched upbringing she was well known to have received at the hands of her neglectful parents, it was in no way unreasonable for her neighbors to think that Tiger would have all kinds of trouble trying to live anything approaching a normal life. Years of abuse, mistreatment, and deprivation during her childhood and youth, they believed, had warped her too much for even as much as a mediocre outcome, much less a rosy one. It is not surprising that neighbors saw her prospects in a dismal light, in view of what she went through as a child. More trouble for the poor girl, they figured, was about all that could be expected.

The overarching challenge of Tiger's life was that

she was never able to overcome the negative tone her own parents established for her existence. Throughout her life, this problem remained a given, even after her mother's mysterious disappearance and the ignominious death of her inexcusably abusive father.

Whenever the subject of Tiger's mother's disappearance was broached with those seniors who provided second-hand information for this account of Mock's life experience, they responded in a manner that would be expected of seniors. In general, they were honest, open, and made no effort to sugar-coat their opinions. It goes without saying that old folks who live in rest homes or in the care of their children do not have much of a reason to hold anything back.

Hardly a one of them held Mock in high esteem, and that is putting it mildly. The bluntly spoken words of a single, exceedingly vocal, uniquely sharp-minded, and unapologetically tart-tongued elderly gentleman are representative of the opinion that prevailed with respect to Mock's behavior as a young woman:

"It was her own insolence and defiance that caused ever damned one of her problems, especially her biggest one of all. The kind of situation that girl got herself into was a hell of a lot bigger deal back then than it is today, and that's the gospel truth of it. Back in her day, a girl who got herself in a fix was up against it, and that's putting it mildly."

"A mess like that sure brought down the wrath of God on a girl in them little country towns like I was raised in. In her situation, even her own neighbors —

the people who normally might have wanted to help her out — didn't want to let her off easy. She dug too deep a hole for herself to get the kind of help she needed when she needed it. That girl was a bridge-burner, that's for damned sure."

"Hell's bells," he offered, "who knows, maybe it's a good thing people was like they were back then. Young people today are too damned casual about having babies, sometimes gettin' married and sometimes not, and then, damn it all, not stayin' married like they are supposed to, even when they do get married, and even if they have kids or not. Nothin' means nothin' to 'um anymore. That's why so damned many marriages end in divorces."

"Anyway," he went on, "it ain't the girl who got herself in trouble, the one they called Mock, the momma, that anybody ought to be talkin' about nowadays. They ought to be talkin' about the other girl, her daughter, the one ever body called Tiger, 'cause of her last name and 'cause she was so feisty. Her momma and her daddy sure as hell done that kid wrong. No wonder she ended up makin' such a damned fool of herself after she growed up."

"Nobody in town had any respect for the girl, no more than they did for her for her daddy Early or her momma Mock, even though it was them that caused most of the kid's problems. That's what you gotta expect," he said, "when parents carry on like her momma and daddy did. Her momma didn't seem to be ashamed of nothin' when she was a kid, even though she damned well shoulda been. More than anything, that's what everbody held against her."

"Besides that," he said, "Mock's own momma and daddy, them Burnhams, never believed a word of what their own daughter said to them, and I'll be damned if I would have either. Sassin' and ignoring what your parents tell you like she did ain't no way for a kid to behave, especially if that kid's a girl. Again, though, what happened to the daughter Tiger is a whole hell of a lot more worth talkin' about than what happened to her mother, Mock. That poor girl never had no chance to live a decent life."

Seniors who knew Mock's story did not have much of anything good say about her, and they felt the same way about her husband Early. For that matter, they did not have anything good to say about their daughter, either. Clearly, though, their most critical comments were directed at Mock. Her own misbehavior over the years had been, as far as they were concerned, the root cause of all the misery that enveloped the family. Although Early was the one who committed an atrocious crime, they did not criticize him a much as they did Mock. Mock, the old folks believed, had put her own foot in the lion's mouth, so it should not have come as any surprise to her that she was bitten.

TIGER BEGINS
LIFE ON HER OWN

SURPRISINGLY, **THE ONLY PERSON** who did not see her future in a negative light after her father Early died unexpectedly in 1904 was Bonnie Tiger herself, not at first, but after thinking things over for a while. True, his passing did knock her back on her heels, but that was no more than a kneejerk reaction; after a reasonable interval, she adapted to her new circumstances much better than expected. That she balked for a shore while should not have come as a surprise anyone, in view of the unnatural and perverse hold her father had had on her for so many years.

The awfulness of the relationship that existed between the two of them was why she at first took the news of his passing as some sort of cruel joke that was being played on her, and that he might not really be dead. She feared that he would show up again later, for no reason other than to bring a whole new raft of miseries into her life. On numerous occasions in the past, he had demonstrated that he was spiteful enough to do things that hateful. Due to his near total domination of her, she thought it would be unwise to put anything past him.

Due to the strength of his hold on her, it took a while for her to mentally confirm that he was truly dead.

Only after attending his dismal funeral and subsequent burial did she finally breathe a first great sigh of relief. It was not a joke, she realized; her father genuinely was dead and gone, and he would not be coming back. He was gone for good. She would never have to slave for or be fearful of him again.

That he really had passed away created something of a vacuum in her daily life at first, a sense of disconnectedness that was not easy to overcome. For a while, she did not know what to do with herself. Her neighbors had asked the very same question she was struggling to answer for herself: What, she wondered, am I going to do from this point forward?

The only viable option open to her, she finally decided, was to continue living in the same isolated household she and her father had lived in since the day she was born. For the moment, she could not conceive of any other way mode of existence. The only way forward for her, she concluded, was to continue doing whatever had to be done to extract a living from the modest estate that had been left in her inexperience hands.

Her father's estate was a meager inheritance indeed, in that everything he left behind was either rundown, nearly depilated, or close to being on its last legs. His property consisted of a scraggly and unkempt plot of communal land, an unpainted old wood frame house that was in extremely poor condition, a few pieces of shoddy furniture, a rag-tag wagon, a couple of well past their prime horses, a few rangy old cows and sheep, an assortment of equally rangy hogs, and a mixed flock of chickens, guinea hens, ducks, and geese. In addition, Tiger located a small stash of cash money that had been hidden at the back of one drawer of his dresser.

Sad no way of knowing that more of an estate had been left behind for her than what was immediately visible, since her father had never shared that kind of information with her. He told her only what he thought she needed to know, and nothing more. As far as she knew, he had no more property than the ragged items she saw before her eyes. Because she didn't know what else to do at that juncture, she accepted her inheritance without question.

On top of the assets that have been enumerated, Tiger had no more real property than a limited wardrobe and the clothes she had on her back. The lump sum value of all of it added together did not amount to much, but to her, because she had never had a single thing to call her own, it seemed like quite a lot. She knew it would have to be enough to get by on, since that was all there was and there would be no more.

For the moment, she was unable to envision any other life for herself than to keep on keeping on, living right where she was and continuing to get by as she had in the past. The life of an isolated, impoverished Indian was all she knew, and, having been kept out of school and raised as much apart from others as her father could get away with, she expected no more than more of the same.

Despite having been left to live alone and totally on her own, one exceptionally welcome thought had taken firm root in her cluttered mind, a thought powerful enough to override any other concern that came up in the wake of her father's passing. The single precious thought that overrode all others was that her daily life was sure to be several orders of magnitude less miserable than it was while her father was alive. Now, she would no longer have to live in fear of his drunken bullying, threats, and eccentricities. It would no longer be mandatory, for example, for her to have to wait on him hand and foot, nor would she ever again have to contend with being terrorized on a whim whenever something she did or failed to do was taken as a sin that deserved to be punished.

The more time she spent thinking about her new reality, the more excited she became. Praise the Lord, she thought to herself; Will wonders never cease? The thought that she would no longer have to worry about being treated like a criminal in her own home was more than merely exciting, it was absolutely exhilarating.

Because she felt like a prisoner who had unexpectedly been released from a long period of confinement, her euphoria knew no bounds. Oh, she knew she would have to find ways of dealing with the practical realities that living on her own would entail, but she felt certain that she would be able to get by very well. Having sole responsibility for doing everything herself was not especially daunting, since nearly every lick of work that had been done in their household in past years had been done by her own hands, and it had been that way for as long as she could remember. Her new life, she figured, would almost certainly be better than it had been in the past, since it could not possibly be any worse.

Tiger was confident, considering what she had had no choice but to do in the past, that she would be able to get by on milk and eggs that would be provided by their rangy domestic animals, vegetables that would be harvested out of their poorly kept garden, any fish or game she could trap or kill, nuts and fruit and berries that could be gathered out of the nearby Deep Fork River bottom, and whatever assistance the federal government doled out to local Indians. These were the sources of sustenance she and her father had lived on for years, and she was confident that they would be more than enough to sustain her in the future, even if she did have to live alone.

The prospect of having to live alone and on their own would have nerved and threatened many young women, but, after she had enough time to think things over, Tiger was not the slightest bit rattled by what lay before her. Essentially, she had been getting by on her own for years, despite having been living with her father, since he had not helped her do much of anything. Doing more of the same was so undaunting that she relished the idea of heading off down the path that lay before her. Enraptured by thoughts of all the many pleasures that were expected to flow from being out from under her father's thumb, she looked forward to being totally on her own. The truth of the matter was that she could hardly wait to get on with it.

After contemplating her prospects for only a few short weeks after her father died, Tiger let her neighbors know that that was exactly what she was going to do. She intended to run her newly inherited household exactly as she wanted to — reporting to no one, catering to no one, and, best of all, without having to bow down to a man who treated her more like an unpaid domestic servant than as a daughter. Who in their right mind, she thought to herself, would miss something like that?

Tiger thought it would be wonderful to be able to select her own pace, so to speak, and to call her own shots as she dealt with the issues the moment. As far as she was concerned, a new life had begun for her, one that seemed almost too good to be true. Her neighbors were skeptical about living alone would work out for her, but she really did not care what they thought. For the first time ever, she could hardly wait to get up in the morning. She thought she was at the beginning of the best of times, not, as many of her neighbors feared might be the case, the very worst. Feeling absolutely exhilarated, she could hardly wait to begin life on her own. Come what may, she decided that she would try to make the best possible hand out the cards that had been dealt to her.

ENTER THE COLONEL,
GEORGE JACKSON CAINE

THE OLD FOLKS who provided information for this account of what happened to Etta Burnham) Tiger after she attended what they referred to as "Mock's Bad Stomp" were dead on right in terms of what they had to say about her daughter Bonnie, or Tiger, as she was called. Unforgivably awful treatment at the hands of her own mother and father had a monumentally terrible effect on the girl. Saying only that she had to endure a life of neglect during her tenderest years and then leaving it there would be unconscionable.

Tiger's case deserves a great deal more attention than cursory coverage; it warrants a special detailed effort on her behalf, solely for the purpose of explaining what became of her after she started life on her own in 1904. It must be told from her perspective, too, not through simply parroting the views of uncomprehending neighbors or local authorities, folks who did nothing but rail against everything she said or did on occasions when they could and should have stepped forward to offer a helping hand. Overhearing comments such as "I couldn't believe my eyes the first time I saw that silly tart parading herself around in that buggy" followed up "there's going to be a bad end for her, there's no doubt about that" had to have rung in her ears like a gong.

Who could blame the girl for wishing a pox on all their houses!

Because her story is one that literally cries out to be told, a sequel to Mock's Bad Stomp is in the works. Entitled "The Disgrace of Colonel Caine," it will be out in a little while, just as soon as it can be made to happen.

ΩΩΩΩ

ALSO BY
MICKEY J. "MIKE" MARTIN

*"Doing Business on the Oklahoma
Land Rush Frontier"
ISBN 9780963827920 (Hardback)
LCCN 95060134*

*"Bryant: A Creek Indian Nation Townsite"
ISBN 9780963827944 (Hardback)
ISBN 9781478198956 (Paperback)
LCCN 2012942764*

*"My Indian Territory School"
ISBN 9780963827968 (Hardback)
ISBN 9781470131098 (Paperback)
LCCN 2012932399*

*"The Lady Luck: Story of the USS LST-864"
ISBN 978-0-9638279-5-2 (Hardback)
LCCN 2003095571*

*****

9 780648 562450